VAMPIRE
HUNTER D

D0933391

Other Vampire Hunter D books published by
DH Press and Digital Manga Publishing

VAMPIRE HUNTER D

VOLUME 6
PILGRIMAGE OF THE SACRED
AND THE PROFANE

Written by

HIDEYUKI KIKUCHI

Illustrations by

YOSHITAKA AMANO

English translation by

KEVIN LEAHY

Milwaukie   Los Angeles

VAMPIRE HUNTER D 6:
PILGRIMAGE OF THE SACRED AND THE PROFANE

Cover art by Yoshitaka Amano

English translation by Kevin Leahy

Book design by Heidi Fainza

Published by
DH Press
a division of Dark Horse Comics
10956 SE Main Street
Milwaukie, OR 97222
dhpressbooks.com

Digital Manga Publishing
1487 West 178th Street, Suite 300
Gardena, CA 90248
dmpbooks.com

Library of Congress Cataloging-in-Publication Data

Kikuchi, Hideyuki, 1949-
  [D--Seima henreki. English]
  Pilgrimage of the sacred and the profane / written by Hideyuki Kikuchi ; illustrated by Yoshitaka Amano ; English translation by Kevin Leahy.
      p. cm. -- (Vampire hunter D ; v. 6)
  ISBN-13: 978-1-59582-106-5
  ISBN-10: 1-59582-106-6
  I. Amano, Yoshitaka. II. Leahy, Kevin. III. Title.
  PL832.I37D313 2006
  895.6'36--dc22

                              2006033348

ISBN-10: 1-59582-106-6
ISBN-13: 978-1-59582-106-5

First DH Press Edition: November 2006
10 9 8 7 6 5 4 3 2 1
Printed in the United States of America
Distributed by Publishers Group West

VAMPIRE HUNTER D

Prologue

S ome called this town the journey's end, others its beginning. Mighty gales blew across the sea of golden sand that stretched from its southern edge. When those mighty winds hit the great gates of steel, pebbles as big as the tip of a child's finger struck them high and low, making the most plaintive sound. It was like a heartrending song sung by someone on the far side of those sands to keep a traveler there.

When the winds were particularly strong, fine sand drifted down on the streets in a drizzle, amplifying the dry creaking of things like the wooden sidewalks and window frames at the saloon. And on very rare occasions, little bugs were mixed in with the sand. Armed with jaws that were tougher than titanium alloy and stronger than a vice, the bugs could chew their way through doors of wood and plastic as if they were paper. Luckily, the petals of faint pink that always came on the heels of the insect invasion killed the bugs on contact—an event that imbued the whole encounter with a kind of elegance. As the order and timing of the arrival of these two forces never varied, the homes in town had to weather the ravages of the tiny killers for only three short minutes.

And yet, on those rare nights when there were great numbers of the bugs, the town was enveloped by a harsh but beautiful hum, like someone strumming on their collective heartstrings. The sound of the bugs' jaws did no harm to humans, and before long the scene would be touched with the flavor of a dream, and then vanish as surely as any dream would on awakening. Some considered it a song of farewell or even a funeral dirge, and people in town grew laconic as the fires in their hearths were reflected in their eyes.

No one knew where the pale pink petals came from. While more than a few had headed off into the desert that was burning-hot even by night, not a single traveler had ever returned. Perhaps they'd reached their destinations, or perhaps their bodies had been buried by the sands, but no word ever came from them. There were some people in town who'd happened to meet such travelers, however, they'd only occasionally be able to raise some fragmented memory of a vaguely remembered face, and then turn their gaze to the gritty winds that ran along the edge of town.

This particular day, the song of the bugs was much sharper than usual and the faint pink rain seemed a bit late, so the townspeople looked out at the streets in the afterglow of sunset with a certain foreboding. The funeral dirge faded, as the time had come for those performing it to die.

And that's when it happened. That's when the young man came to town.

The Hidden

I

The sound of the bugs grew more intense, and the men encamped around the tables and seated at the bar turned their fierce gazes toward the door. Grains of sand became a length of silk that blew in and then almost instantly broke apart to trace wind-wrought swirls on the floor. The door was shut again.

Eyes swimming with indecision caught the new arrival. Was this someone they could take in, or should the newcomer be kept out?

It took a little while before the floorboards began to creak. Time needed to decide which direction to creak off in. Done.

The piano stopped; the pianist had frozen. The coquettish chatter of the women petered out. The men's noisy discussions ceased. Behind the bar, the bartender had gone stiff with a bottle of booze in one hand and a glass in the other. There was curiosity and fear about just what was going to happen next.

A table to the left of the door and a bit toward the back was the newcomer's destination. Two figures were settled around it—one in black, the other in blue. Wearing an ebony silk hat and a mourning coat with a hem that looked like it reached his ankles, one evoked a mortician. The deep-blue, brimless cap and the shirt of the same color that covered the powerful frame of the other were undoubtedly crafted from the hide of the blue jackal, considered by many to be the most vicious beast on the Frontier. Both men were slumped in their chairs with their heads hung low as if they were sleeping.

The source of the creaking footsteps surely noticed something very unusual about the situation—all the other tables around the pair were devoid of customers. It was as if they were being avoided. As if they were despised. As if they frightened people. Another odd thing—it wasn't a whiskey bottle and glasses that sat on the table before them. Black liquid pooled in the bottom of their brass coffee cups, which still had swirls of white steam lovingly hovering over their rims.

Even after the creaking stopped, the two men didn't lift their heads, but every other sound in the place died when the footsteps ended. Several seconds of silence settled. Then a taut voice shattered the stillness.

"We don't take kindly to folks with no manners, kid!" the figure in blue said.

And immediately after that—

"Your mistake, Clay," the other one remarked, his very voice so steeped in black that it made everyone else in the small watering hole tremble.

"Well, I'll be," the first man said, his blue cap rising unexpectedly to reveal his eyes; set in his steely face, they were even bluer than his attire. Though he'd called the person he heard walking over a kid, he was only about twenty years old himself. His face looked mean enough to kill a timid man with one glare, but he suddenly smiled innocently and said, "They say you can disguise your face, but you can't do a thing about how old your steps sound."

"Too bad, sonny," the newcomer said. The voiced spilled from lips like dried-out clay, as cracked and creased as the rest of his face. More than the countenance so wrinkled that age could no longer be determined, more than the silver hair tied back with a vermilion ribbon, it was the slight swell in the gold-fringed vest and blouse that gave away the sex of the speaker. "I happen to hate being ignored," she continued. "I don't care if you're the biggest thing to ever happen to the Outer Frontier; I still think you ought to show your elders the proper respect. Don't you agree?"

The rest of the customers remained as still as statues. Even so, an excited buzz filled the room. Suddenly, someone said, "That old lady's looking to start a fight with Bingo and Clay Bullow!"

"What do you want?" Clay asked. His tone was incredibly light.

"Well, tomorrow, I'm heading across the desert to the Inner Frontier. And I want the two of you to come with me."

Clay's mouth dropped open. Without taking his eyes off the crone, he said, "Hey, bro—some old hag I don't even know says she wants us to keep her company on a trip through the desert."

"There'd be a heap of pay in it for you," the crone told him. "I'd like you to watch out for me and another person, you see. With you two along, I figure we'd get there in less than a week. . . and alive, to boot."

"Bro—"

"You don't know her, you say?" another voice said. Calling to mind rough-hewn rock, his tone didn't exactly match his spindly, spider-like limbs. "Little brother, you'd best jiggle that memory of yours a bit more. We might not have met her, but we know her name. You'll have to pardon me," he told the old woman, "but I'm asleep at the moment. Wish I could greet you properly, Granny Viper, People Finder."

The silent saloon was rocked. She was Granny Viper: the chances that the Inner Frontier's greatest locator of those who'd been hidden would run into the Outer Frontier's greatest fighters had to be about ten-million-to-one. They were really in luck.

"I couldn't care less about greetings. So, how about it? What's your answer?" the old woman chirped like a bird.

"We're waiting for someone," the face beneath the silk hat replied.

"Whoever it is, I'm sure they'll be dead before they get here." The crone's mouth twisted into an evil hole. Her maw was a black pit—without a single tooth in it. "And if they do make it here, they're gonna have a little run-in with you, I suppose. Either way, it's the same thing, am I right?"

"Without a doubt," Clay said, throwing his head back with a huge laugh. "But this time, we've got a real job cut out for ourselves. Depending on how things go, we might end up—" Staring at the back of the hand that'd appeared before him without warning, Clay caught himself. "I know, bro—I've said too much already."

Bingo's right hand slowly retracted.

"Sure you're not interested?" the crone asked in a menacing tone.

The man in the silk hat didn't answer.

"Sorry, but I just *have* to have you two along," Granny insisted.

The wall of men and women around the trio receded anxiously, and all eyes focused on the hands of the old woman and the two brothers. In light of what was about to happen, it was a completely natural thing to do. Their gazes were filled with consternation— even an old woman like Granny Viper had to have some sort of "weapon" if she lived out on the Frontier. Her lower back looked like it'd snap in two if someone even touched it, and just below it she wore a survival belt with a number of pouches on it. Still she had no bowie knife or machete—the most basic of equipment. But what everyone's eyes were drawn to was a large jar that looked like it was ceramic. It had an opening that seemed wide enough to easily accommodate the fist of a giant man, but it was stoppered with a polymer fiber lid. And although it looked like it would be fairly heavy even if it were empty, the old woman walked and stood as if unconcerned with its weight. One of the taller spectators had been up on the tips of his toes for a while trying to get a good look at it, but the lid was the same gray color as the jar, and its contents were completely hidden from view.

Similarly, the weapons of the two men were every bit as eccentric as hers. What hung at the right hip of the younger brother, Clay, couldn't have been any more inappropriate for him—a golden harp strung with silver strings. As for the older brother, Bingo, what he carried was more surprising than anything. He was completely unarmed.

"Granny Viper, People Finder" and "The Fighting Bullow Brothers." Getting a sense that an otherworldly conflict never meant for human eyes was about to be joined here between some of the Frontier's most renowned talents—and the weird weapons they possessed—the saloon patrons were all seized by the silence of the grave. The crone's right hand slowly dropped to her jar. At the same time, Clay's hand reached for the harp on his hip. Bingo didn't budge an inch. And just as the three deadly threads were about to silently twist together . . .

The black bowler hat flew up in the air. The wrinkled face of the crone looked back over her shoulder. The gaze of the youth in blue was there just a second later, at the door. Closed since the crone entered, the door now had the eyes of all three of these rough customers trained on it. There was no one there—at least, not in front of it—so what were the three of them looking at?

At just that moment the door knob turned. Hinges squealing as they bit down on sand, the door became an expanding domain of darkness on the wall. Perhaps the figure it revealed had been born of the very night itself. The saloon patrons backed away, and the hue of the black garments that covered all but his pale and perfect countenance made it seem that he blew in like a fog of fine sand. As if the countless eyes on him meant nothing, the young man shut the door behind him and headed over to the bar. What they were dealing with now was something even more unusual than the Bullow Brothers or Granny Viper, People Finder. With every step forward the figure in black took, grains of sand dropped from his long coat. To the women in the bar, even these seemed to sparkle darkly. As soon as the young man stopped at the bar, the people heard him say in a voice like steel, "There's supposed to be someone here by the name of Thornton."

Swallowing hard, the bartender nodded. Though he was big enough to serve as the bouncer too, the man's colossal frame grew stiff. It sounded like he was barely squeezing the words out as he said, "You're Mr. D . . . aren't you?"

No reply was needed. Though the bartender had only heard about one characteristic of the Hunter, he knew this was unquestionably the man who stood before him.

"He's out back right now," the bartender said, raising his right hand to point the way. "But he's having himself a little *entertainment* at the moment." It was common knowledge that in many cases, Frontier town saloons also doubled as whorehouses.

D walked off in the direction the man had indicated. He'd gone about a dozen steps when someone said to him, "It's a pleasure to meet you."

It was Bingo.

"Bingo Bullow is the name. That's my younger brother, Clay. You might've heard of us. I was thinking we might get to know the greatest Vampire Hunter on the Frontier."

Bingo looked at the back of the figure who'd halted his step. Like his body, the elder Bullow's face was extremely thin, and his chin was covered by a wild growth of beard. Seemingly hewn from rock, his expression shifted just a bit then.

As if he'd merely stopped there on a whim, D started walking again.

"Well, shut my mouth!" Granny Viper exclaimed in an outrageously loud voice, indifferent to all the other spectators. "This *is* a surprise. I didn't know there was a man alive who'd turn his back on Bingo Bullow when he offers an invite. I like your style! Indeed, I do!"

"Hold it, you!" Clay shouted as if trying to destroy the old woman's words. He jumped to his feet. His cruel young face grew red as hot blood rushed to his head. As he reached for his elegant weapon with his right hand, another, thinner hand—that of his brother—pressed against his stomach stopping him.

"Knock it off," Bingo told him.

The older brother's word must've been law, because the younger Bullow didn't utter a single complaint after that, and the anger that radiated from his powerful form rapidly dispersed.

"I'll be waking up soon," the elder Bullow informed him. "We'll have to wait until the next time I'm asleep to pay our respects."

Out of the countless eyes there, only those of the crone sparkled.

The door to the back room opened and then closed again, swallowing the darkness given human form in the process.

The cramped room was filled with a lascivious aroma. Long, thin streams of smoke rose from an opening in the metallic urn that sat on the round table. It was an aphrodisiac unique to the Frontier sectors, and all who smelled the scent—young or old, male or female—were transformed into lust-crazed beasts. On the other side of the table sat an ostentatious bed that'd been slathered with the gaudiest color of paint imaginable, and on that bed something terribly alluring wriggled: a knot of naked women, all of them dripping with sweat. It was probably the influence of the aphrodisiac that kept them from so much as turning to look at the intruder as he entered.

Perhaps wondering what was going on outside the intertwined flesh, a raven-haired head popped out of the middle of that pale pile of femininity even as feverish panting continued to fill the air. From the man's face, it was impossible to tell whether he was young or middle-aged. He must've been the only one who'd responded to D's knock. Roughly pushing his way free of the women clinging to him, he finally stopped what he was doing, and stared directly at D.

"Well, I'll be . . . Just goes to show you can't believe everything you hear, I guess. Your looks are so good, my hair's practically standing on end." And then, as he hastily began shoving the women out of the way, he hissed, "C'mon, move it!"

Although his squat form looked to be less than five feet tall, he had a considerable amount of fat on him—evidence of days spent in pursuit of culinary delights. He didn't bother to cover himself as he slipped on his underpants. Once the man was wrapped in a robe, he actually looked quite dignified. Digging a thick pair of glasses out of his coat pocket, he put them on. He almost looked like he could pass for a scholar from the Capital.

"This isn't exactly the most appropriate place to receive a guest who's traveled so far, but, you see, I wasn't expecting to see you so soon." Glancing then at the electric clock on the wall, he added, "Actually, you're right on time. But back at the hotel, I heard that a cloud of moving miasma had shown up on the road, and that no one would be able to get through for a couple of days . . . Guess I should've remembered I was dealing with the Vampire Hunter D."

In what was surely a rare occurrence for the young Hunter, he received a somewhat sheepish smile from the other man, but when the man in black failed to move even a single muscle in his face, Thornton shrugged his shoulders and said, "Well, I suppose I should tell you about the job, then."

The reason he averted his gaze at this point wasn't so much to change the tone of the conversation, but rather because he'd reached the point where he could no longer stand looking at D head-on. Regardless of gender, those who gazed at the young man's gorgeous visage for too long began to hallucinate that they were being drawn into the depths of his eyes. Actually, the women that Thornton had shoved out of the way had been ready to voice their dissatisfaction when D suddenly entered their field of view and left them frozen with their mouths agape.

"Okay, get your asses out of here! I'll pay you twice what you had coming," the little man—Thornton—said, but even as he shoved them out, the women kept their dumbstruck gazes trained on D until the very end.

"Care for a drink?" Thornton asked the Hunter as he picked up the bottle of liquor sitting on the table, but then he shrugged his shoulders. "Oh, that's right—you dhampirs like to say, 'I never drink wine,' don't you? Sorry. I may be a lawyer, but I'm still just a plain old human. Pardon me while I have one."

Filling his glass to the very brim with the amber liquid, Thornton pressed it to his lips. Time and again, his Adam's apple bobbed up and down before he exhaled roughly and set his empty glass back on the table.

As he nervously brought his hand up to wipe his lips, Thornton began by saying, "I wrote to you for one purpose and one purpose alone. I want you to cross the desert. To go all the way to the town of Barnabas, across this 'Desert of No Return' where so many have never been seen again."

"For what purpose?" D asked, opening his mouth at last. "In your letter, you said you could furnish me with information about someone I have a great interest in."

"That's correct," Thornton said, nodding his agreement. "And the reason I can do so is because the request to send you out into the desert comes from that very person."

II

Now that it was late at night, the sound of the bugs had only increased in its plaintive rhapsody. A few minutes later, blossoms covered the town and the sounds died out, began anew, and then vanished again . . . as if the night would never end, and the song of parting would never cease.

It was at that moment that a wrinkled hand knocked on the door to a room in a hotel on the edge of town. There was no answer. Without waiting very long, the hand pushed against the door. It opened easily. The interior was claimed by the same shade of darkness as the world outside. The reason Granny Viper turned to the right side without hesitation wasn't because she'd memorized the location of the bed, but because she could see as well in the dark as she could at midday.

"Pardon the intrusion," the old woman called out in a hoarse voice, and although she received no reply to her greeting, she could see the tall figure that lay on the bed clearly enough. "Ordinarily, I'd call you careless, but for the Vampire Hunter D, having the door locked or unlocked probably makes no difference. Anyone who came in here with evil in mind wouldn't live to tell about it." Her tone was buoyant, and she meant her words as a compliment. As always, there was no reply, so the hunched-over figure said, "Sure, I'd heard of you before, but I never could've imagined you'd be so incredible. Obviously, you're awful good-looking, too, but what I couldn't believe was that someone actually ignored the Bullow Brothers. That's when I thought to myself: *That settles it.* At first, I was aiming to ask the two of them to help, but forget that now. Who needs a couple of punks fresh outta short pants, anyway? I've decided to go with you instead."

Here the old woman paused and waited for the Hunter to respond, but there was no reply. Perhaps he was just a shadow that had taken human form? She strained her ears and still she couldn't hear him draw a single breath, nor could she catch the beating of his heart. The crone realized that if her night vision wasn't so keen, she'd never have noticed his presence.

Any ordinary person would've lost hope at this exercise in futility, or grown indignant at his cold-heartedness. But the old woman went on talking. "When I first came in," she said, "I didn't feel the urge to kill from you, and I don't now, either. I've been to other Hunters' rooms, but it's unbelievable. They're always on edge, never knowing when somebody's gonna try and get the drop on them, and you can feel the violence just hanging around in the air outside their rooms. No matter how big they are, *you're* above them all. If someone came in here, they'd take you for a stone until the second you struck them dead. On the other hand, if you wanted to, you could stop a foe cold through a stone wall with just a harsh look in their direction. But I suppose I'd be surprised if you had a mind to do that even once in your life. And that's why I've pinned all my hopes on you."

In a manner of speaking, all the old woman's efforts were rewarded.

"What do you want with me?" asked the shadow of all shadows.

"I already told you, didn't I? I want you to come with me. You know, across the desert to the town of Barnabas. There'd be a nice piece of change in it for you. Enough for all the booze and broads you'd ever want. I just know you couldn't say no to a sweet deal like this."

"No." His concise reply had an intensity that completely severed the discussion.

"Well, why the hell not?"

"Leave."

"Stop mucking around," Granny said to him. "I just told you how set I am on having you. Maybe you think you're too good to listen to some old bag, eh? Well, I'll show you. You might not think so, but I'm pretty well known across the Frontier. And while they may not be quite as dangerous as you, I know a lot of people—folks that'll come running just as soon as I give the word. No matter how tough you are, up against a hundred of them—"

The crone's voice died there. As if pushed by something, her stooped figure leapt back. Perhaps unable to weather the other-worldly air that staggered the imagination, she flew out of the room with terrific speed. Light flowed in from the corridor.

"Stop it," Granny shouted. Her words had the ring of an entreaty. "What, do you plan on killing me? I'm more than a hundred years old, you know! What'll you do if you give me a heart attack or something?"

Yet the unearthly air continued to creep toward her.

"Just stop it, or this kid—this girl—will die, too!" she shouted, slipping around the door and reappearing in the rectangular space pushing another figure. Someone with eyes that could pierce the darkness would see the shoulder-length black hair and the soft lines beneath the simple flesh-tone dress, and might even determine that the girl was about seventeen or eighteen years old. Without saying a single word, she just squatted there, hugging her own shoulders. The Hunter's ghastly aura was merciless.

"Please, stop," the crone cried out from behind the door. "The girl's name is Tae—she was one of *the hidden*. What's more, it was the Nobility that hid her!"

The girl's rigid body collapsed unexpectedly. Bracing one hand against the floor, she heaved a few short, sharp gasps. Rather attractive in its own way, her face was as expressionless as stone now, as if it terrified her to draw even the smallest of breaths. The girl seemed to have the world crushing in on her from all sides.

Granny's face peeked around from behind the door as her expression turned deadly serious. She came out slowly, moving with a weighty and plaintive gait. Circling around behind Tae, she put her hands on the girl's pale shoulders. Turning to the darkened depths of the room, she asked, "Do you know what my trade is?" Quickly realizing she wasn't likely to get a reply, she said, "I'm a people finder. I've been nicknamed Viper, like the snake, but I'm not one of them dala-a-dozen orphan trackers they've got hanging around here. I specialize in children who've been taken—I find *the hidden*. You know," she said to the Hunter, "I can't very well stand out here talking about it. Let me come back in for a second. C'mon, stand up," she told the Tae as she forced her to her feet, went back into the room, and closed the door. What's more, she then pulled out a chair, told Tae, "Have a seat," and settled herself in another chair, in a display that took presumptuousness to laudable heights. And yet, the reason she didn't complain about D's rudeness as he continued to just lie there was because his ghastly aura still permeated her flesh. "This girl—" she began to explain before she was interrupted.

The darkness was split by the voice of its master. "You mentioned the Nobility, didn't you?"

"Why, yes, I do believe I did," the old woman said, fighting back her delight. "She's a genuine, bona fide victim of hiding by the Nobility. I nearly killed myself getting her out of Castle Gradinia."

For all the supernatural phenomena that occurred out on the Frontier, the notion of *the hidden* had an especially chilling connotation. Unlike profit-motivated kidnappings, these could suddenly happen right out in public or under conditions where it should've been impossible to just vanish. The victims could be young or old, male or female, but in the case of young ladies it was almost certain to conjure images of a dreaded fate that would make anyone quake with terror . . . even as it robbed them of their tears. There were several possible causes for these disappearances, and they were sometimes attributed to unknown creatures or to the dimensional rips that appeared at irregular intervals. But in cases where members of the Nobility were suggested as the culprits, the terror sprang not from the disappearance itself, but from the anticipated result. What kind of fate might befall a young lady in such a situation? If they were merely prey to satisfy their captor's taste for blood, they might be saved. Luckier still were those who were given positions as maidservants on the whim of the Nobility, though this was less common. A fair number of girls were rescued under those circumstances, but there could be more to it than that . . .

"A hell of a time I had there," Granny said, twisting her lips. "I was thinking I'd taken out all their defensive systems, but there was still one left. Damned thing put me to sleep until night. Well, I'd already made up my mind about what I was gonna do, so I drove a stake through the bastard's heart just as he was getting out of his coffin. Still, he was thrashing around like nobody's business, and I had to keep that accursed stake stuck in him for a good three hours before he simmered down. After that, I searched the place, and happened to find this girl. Not to worry, though, I've checked her out, and as far as I can tell, there's nothing wrong with her. I had her hypnotized so deeply it would've driven her mad to go any further. And, naturally, she can walk around in daylight."

"How did you find her?" D asked, his query free of inflection.

Tae shivered with fear.

The crone shrugged her shoulders and said, "There really wasn't much to it. Once I went down into the basement, I found a prison where they kept humans. She was locked in there. I asked her a few things, and by the sound of it, they had her slaving away as a maid of sorts. You can guess the rest. She was still right in the head, so she remembered which village she hails from. The sheriff in Gradinia even had a request from her parents to look for her.

And that's how I ended up transporting her. That's what I do, you know." Granny nodded in a way that made it clear she was quite proud of what she did, too.

"And the Noble—what was his name?"

The old woman didn't answer that question. Although the Hunter's tone and the direction he faced hadn't changed, the crone understood that this query was directed at Tae.

Tae's body trembled, but her face remained aimed at the floor. She didn't say a word. It was almost as if she was erecting shields of incredible density all around herself.

The old woman, however, grew agitated and barked, "What are you doing? Hurry up and answer the man! This could mean the difference between us getting to the town of Barnabas safely or not!"

Tae said nothing.

"Oh, you stupid little twit!" Granny shouted, raising her right hand violently while keeping her back as straight as an arrow. Apparently, her hunching had been part of an act to get his sympathy, but there was no need for her to follow through with the blow.

"Leave," D said, making it clear that their visit had concluded.

"Wait just one second. I'm not done speaking my piece yet," the crone cried out in a pitiful tone. There wasn't an iota of the bluster she'd shown the Bullow Brothers left in her voice. The sudden and complete reversal was a nice change, though. "Like I just explained, we're in a situation where we've gotta get across the desert . . . and we've got a time limit, too. If we don't make it in four days, counting tomorrow, we're out of luck. See, the girl's family is in the town of Barnabas, but on the morning of the fifth day, they'll be moving on to somewhere else. Given the size of the desert, it's gonna be a close call. If we were to go around it, it'd take us more than a week, which is why we definitely need us some heavy-duty backup. Now, I don't know just what brings you to town, but if you haven't taken care of whatever it is, I'd like you to put it off for a while and come along with us. I don't care whether you wanna do it or not; I've already settled on you. Hell, even the girl said she likes you. Didn't you, sweetie?" the crone said, seeking some corroboration, but the girl remained as stiff as a board. "See what I mean? She likes you so much that she's at a loss for words. Of course, that's only natural, you being so handsome and all." Chuckling, she added, "This may sound strange, but if I was a tad younger myself, I don't think I could keep away from you, stud."

Of course, D didn't move a muscle.

Seeing that this was having no effect, Granny changed tactics. Her tone suddenly became tearful. Sobs echoed through the darkness. "Have you no pity for this poor child?" she asked, her entreaty coming in a nasal tone. "She was only ten when she was taken, and she spent eight years locked up in a Noble's castle. Even I don't know what happened to her during all that time—and I'm not about to ask. Can you blame me? Somehow, though, the girl survived. That's right—she kept herself alive for eight long years, a girl all alone in a world we can scarcely imagine. Doesn't she have the right to live the rest of her life in happiness now? When I found out her family was still alive and well, it brought tears to my eyes, I tell you. Her life's just about to begin. Now, wouldn't you wanna do everything in your power to help her out?" Winded from her speech, Granny caught her breath. Tears glistened in her eyes. It was all terribly impressive.

D's answer was brief: "Leave." The word had a forceful ring to it.

The crone was about to say something, but decided against it. "Okay, I get the message," she spat back in a rancorous tone that would've raised the eyebrows of all who heard it. "I'm gonna call it a night, but there's no way we're giving up on this. We need you. I don't care what I've gotta stoop to; I'm gonna get you to come along with us. C'mon, Tae."

As she indignantly turned to the door, the old woman cursed in a low voice. Her back suddenly hunched over again. Taking the girl with downcast eyes by the hand, Granny dragged her out into the hall and disappeared.

The door closed with a force that shook the room. The reverberations were absorbed then by the air and building materials, and mere seconds later, when silence once again ruled the darkness, the chirping began. It was the small and distant sound of the bugs pecking at the dark of night, scratching at the hearts of all who listened. It was the sort of sound that made those who heard it want to lie down deep in the earth. To those who were leaving town, the songs seemed to bid them adieu. Who knows how many listeners likened the melody the bugs continued to play to a funeral dirge. The sound continued just a little while longer, and soon, outside the room's tiny window, the light pink petals began to rain down. Yet even then, the figure lying on the bed did nothing, as if melodies of parting and funeral laments held no relevance for him.

III

The next day, the world belonged to the winds. Every time they whistled forlornly, a thin coat of what looked like gold dust was thrown onto the streets.

It was still early morning when the angry voices surrounded the hotel. The number of people around the building and packed into its lobby looked like it encompassed the entire population of the small town. They demanded that the hotel manager chase off the Vampire Hunter that was staying there immediately, and although he was reluctant at first, he consented after hearing all the circumstances. And while he understood the reasons, his heart must've been heavy at the thought of dealing with the greatest Hunter on earth, because his steps were sluggish as he headed to the stairs from the front desk.

All of the townspeople behind the manager were armed. Although there was usually comfort in numbers, the reason their faces were as pale as paper was because they, like all residents of the Frontier, were well-informed about the general capabilities of Hunters. The fingers wrapped around their stake-firing guns and long spears were stiff, cold, and clammy.

It was probably the manager's good fortune that he didn't have to knock on the door in the end. The door creaked open before his trembling hand, and the room's occupant appeared. As that handsome countenance silently watched them, the townspeople forgot their murderous rage and were left dazed. But it was the manager who noticed D was prepared to set off on a trip. Bringing his hand to his heart in relief, he asked, "Will you be leaving, sir?"

"I can't rest here any longer." D's eyes gazed quietly at the men filling the hallway. The lust for violence that'd churned there had already disappeared, and they were gripped now by a sort of lethargy—just from a single glance from the Hunter. As D walked ahead, the mass of people broke to either side, as if pushed back by some unseen agent. The only thing showing in the eyes of the men pressed against the wall was fear. D went down the stairs. The lobby was a crucible of furious humanity. Like the sea in days of old, they parted right down the middle, opening a straight path between the Vampire Hunter and the door.

"Your bill has been paid," the manager called from behind him.

D went outside. In the street, there was a furry of wind and people—and eyes steeped in hatred and fear. Just as he took hold of the reins to his cyborg horse in the shack next to the hotel, a cheerful voice called out to him.

"Scaring the hell out of a group that size is quite a feat," Clay Bullow said, donning a carefree smile, but D didn't even look at him as he got up in the saddle. "Hold up. We're leaving, too. Why don't you come with us?" Clay suggested, seeming just a bit flustered. The hot-headedness of the previous night had burned away like a fog. He was also on horseback, with the reins in his hands. "My brother's waiting at the edge of town. You know, I'm not talking about us all being friends or nothing. We wanna settle up with you."

As D casually rode off, Clay gave a kick to his mount's flanks and headed after him. Flicking the reins, he pulled up on D's left side.

"Now, this is a surprise! Guess I should've expected no less," he said, eyes going wide. His exclamation was entirely sincere. "You draw your sword over your right shoulder. If you leave me on your left, you can't try to cut me without turning your horse and everything this way. Have you got so much confidence that you don't care about something like that, or are you just plain stupid? Just so you know, this is my good side."

By that, Clay must've meant the hand he'd use to fight. His harp was on his right hip. His hand glided toward the strings.

"Care to try me?" the Hunter asked.

Clay's hand froze in midair. All it had taken was that one question from D. The Hunter was rocking back and forth on his horse.

The people saw Clay's mount halt, and the other rider rode away at a leisurely pace.

D turned the corner. The great gates that separated the town from the desert were hazy through the clouds of sand. They lay straight ahead of him. D advanced without saying a word.

Massive forms challenged the sky to either side of the gate—enormous trees that were the deepest shade of blue. Looking like thousands of giant serpents twisted together, the trunk of each had countless cracks running through it. There were no smaller branches or twigs. Naturally, there were no leaves, either. The two colossal trees had died ages ago. Beside the huge tree on the right, a figure in a silk hat sat on a horse, and next to the tree on the left rested a wagon with a cylindrical cover. Covered on three sides by a canopy of reinforced plastic, the driver's seat was occupied by Granny Viper and Tae. All of them were waiting for D—but the Hunter rode by without glancing at either party.

"My younger brother was supposed to go collect you," Bingo said. Perhaps he was still "sleeping," as his face was turned to the ground under his black bowler hat. As he spoke in his sleep, his voice seemed unbounded. "But I guess the Hunter D was a little too much baggage for him to handle after all," the elder Bullow continued. "Someday, we'd like some of your time to settle things

nice and leisurely. We're headed down the same road you are. What do you say to going with us?"

Granny Viper cackled like a bird of prey, blowing aside the dusty clouds. "You think our young friend here travels with anyone else? Looks like the Fighting Bullow Brothers have gone soft in the head! He's always on his own. He was born alone, lives alone, and he'll die alone. One look at him should be enough to tell you as much."

The crone turned an enraptured gaze on the pale profile riding past her. "But this time," she said to the Hunter, "I need you to make an exception. Now, I don't know what you're up to, but if you're going across the desert, then Barnabas is the only place you could be headed . . . which happens to be where we're headed, too. Even if you don't want to come with us, we still have the right to follow along after you." Glaring in Bingo's direction, she added, "Sheesh. I don't know what you boys are trying to prove, but we could do without you. I'm giving you fair warning," she said to Bingo in a tone that could cow even a giant of a man. "If you make a move against D, I'll take it as a move against *us*. Try anything funny, and you'll find yourselves with more than one foe on your hands."

And then the crone pulled back on her reins. An electrical current passed through the metallic rings looped around the necks of the four cyborg horses in her team, triggering the release of adrenaline. A hot and heavy wind smacked the horses in the nose as they hit the street. Beyond the great gates that opened to either side, D's shape was dwindling in the distance. The wagon was close behind him, and Bingo's horse was about a minute behind the wagon. Another five minutes later, Clay passed through the gate as well. As soon as he'd gone, a sad sound began to ring out all over town. If the wind was a song that bid them farewell, then the cries of the bugs were a funeral dirge. And before long, even that died out.

The crone's covered wagon soon pulled up on D's right-hand side. Golden terrain stretched on forever, and the sky was a leaden hue. The thick canopy of clouds that shrouded the desert was almost never pierced by the rays of the sun; in the last fifty years or so, the sun had only been seen once. Somewhere out on the line that divided heaven from earth, a few ribbon-like beams of light had once burst through the sea of clouds in a sight that was said to be beautiful beyond compare. Some even said there was a town out where it'd shone. But after that, the light was never seen again.

"Oh my, looks like those two really are coming along," Granny said after adjusting her canopy and peering into the omni-directional safety mirror. Made of more than a dozen lenses bent into special angles and wired in place, the mirror not only provided clear views of all four sides of the wagon, but of the sky above it and earth below as well. The figures that appeared in the lens that covered the back, of course, were the Bullow Brothers. "Why do you reckon they're following you?" the crone asked as she wiped the sweat from her brow. Though sunlight didn't penetrate the clouds, the heat had no trouble getting through. In fact, the inescapable swelter was a special characteristic of this desert. "They say a fighter's blood starts pumping faster when he finds someone tougher than him. Well," she laughed, "it sure as hell ain't anything as neat as all that. You know why you were thrown out of that hotel?"

D didn't answer her. Most likely, it was all the same to him. He'd probably have just left his lodging at checkout time. No matter what the townspeople tried, it wouldn't have mattered, because in truth, they wouldn't have been able to do anything to him.

The old woman looked to the heavens in disgust. "Unbelievable! The mob back in town was ready to kill you. You must've known as much. And yet you mean to tell me you don't even wanna know *why*?"

Waiting a while for an answer, the old woman finally shrugged her shoulders.

"Watch out for those two, you hear me? The reason everyone in town was after you is because the daughter of some farmer out on the edge of town had her blood drained last night. They've probably got her in isolation by now, but when they found her in that state this morning, they just jumped to the conclusion you were to blame. After all, you are the world-famous Vampire Hunter D. And you're a 100 percent genuine dhampir."

As Granny said this, she took her left hand off the reins, got the canteen that sat by her feet, and brought it to her mouth. The temperature continued to climb rapidly—a sure sign that the world humans inhabited was now far away.

"Now, I can tell with just one look at you that you're not that kind of weak-willed, half-baked Noble, but the world don't work that way. Everyone got all steamed-up and figured it was entirely your fault, which is why they formed that big ol' mob. Hell, they don't even know for sure if she was even bitten or not. Truth is . . . any quack in town could've easily made a wound that'd look like that. Give the girl a shot of anesthetic, and she'd have the same symptoms as if one of the Nobility fed on her, and she wouldn't be able to eat for four or five days, either. It was them," the crone said, tossing her jaw in the direction of the Bullow brothers. "They did it. To get you thrown out."

Seeing a slight movement of D's lips, the old woman had to smother a smile of delight.

"Why would they want me thrown out of town?" the Hunter asked, though from his tone it was completely uncertain whether or not he was actually interested. It was like the voice of the wind, or a stone. Given the nature of the young man, the wind seemed more likely.

"I wouldn't have the slightest notion about that," the crone said, smirking all the while. "You should ask them. After all, they're following along after you. But it's my hope that you'll hold off on any fighting till our journey's safely over. I don't wanna lose my precious escort, you see."

Not seeming upset that he'd been appointed her guardian at some point, D said, "Soon."

The word startled the old woman. "What, you mean something's coming? Been across this desert before, have you?"

"I read the notes written by someone who crossed it a long time ago," D replied, his eyes staring straight ahead.

There was no breeze, just endless crests of gray and gold. The temperature had passed a hundred and five. The crone was drenched with sweat.

"If the contents are to be believed, the man who kept that notebook made it halfway across," D continued.

"And that's where he met his death, eh? What killed him?"

"When I found him, his arm was poking out from some rocks, with his notebook still clutched in his hand even though he was just a skeleton."

The old woman shrugged. "At any rate, it probably won't do us much good, right? I mean, you must've gone as far as he did."

"When I found him, he was out in the middle of the Mishgault stone stacks."

Granny's eyes bulged. "That's more than three thousand miles from here. You don't say . . . So, that's how it goes, eh? The seas of sand play interesting games, don't they? What should we do, then?"

"Think for yourself."

"Now I'll—" the old woman said, about to fly into a rage, but a semitransparent globe drifted before her. The front canopy was in the woman's way, so she touched its curved plastic surface and it quickly retracted to the rear.

The thing was about a foot-and-a-half in diameter. It was perfectly round, too. Within it, a multicolored mass that seemed to be a liquid was gently rippling.

"A critter of some sort," Granny remarked. "I've never seen anything like it before. Tae, get inside."

Once she'd sent the girl into the depths of the covered wagon, the crone took the nearby blunderbuss and laid it across her lap. With a muzzle that flared like the end of a trumpet, the weapon would launch a two-ounce ball of lead with just a light squeeze of its trigger. Pulling out the round it already contained, the old woman took a scattershot shell from the tin ammo box that sat by the weapon and loaded that instead. Her selection was based merely on a gut feeling, but it was a good choice. From somewhere up ahead of them, more globes than they could count began to surround the wagon and the rider.

"Looks like the Bullow Brothers are gonna wet themselves," the old woman laughed as she eyed one of the lenses in her mirror. "What the hell are those critters, anyway?"

"I don't know," D said simply.

"What do you mean?! Didn't you just say they'd be attacking us *soon?*"

"There was nothing about them in the notebook."

The crone's eyes went wide. "Then this is something new, is it?"

The question was barely off the old woman's tongue when their surroundings were filled with light. Not only had the globes taken on strange colors, but they'd begun pulsing with life.

"God, these things are disgusting. I'm gonna make a break for it!" Granny shouted, forgetting all about the man she'd asked to guard them as she worked the reins for all she was worth. The cyborg horses in her team kicked up the ground in unison. The intense charge pushed the globes out of the way, leaving them spinning wildly in the vehicle's wake. Racing on for a good four hundred feet, the crone then stopped her wagon. As her eyes came to rest on D by their side, she was all smiles.

"Stuck right with us, didn't you?" Granny said to him. "Forget what you said—I just knew you'd be worried about the two of us. Good thing for us. That's just what I like to see in a strong man."

The old woman was about to lavish even more praise on the Hunter when suddenly she stopped. D had taken one hand and slowly pointed to their rear. "Take a shot at them," he said in a low voice. Perhaps he'd only kept up with her to see what effect it would have.

Though her face made no secret of her apprehension, Granny must've shared his interest, because she raised her blunderbuss.

"Oh my," she said. "Those two boys are coming, too. Hold on a minute."

"Now," the Hunter told her.

"What?" said the old woman, her eyes widening. She then found out why D had instructed her to shoot—the globes they'd knocked out of the way were now rising without a sound to disappear in the high heavens. They were moving so quickly that hitting them would be no easy task, even with scattershot. The globes that surrounded the galloping Bullow Brothers also broke off immediately and headed for the sky.

"You are one scary character," Granny muttered, not exaggerating her opinion of him in the slightest. And as she spoke, she brought the blunderbuss to her shoulder and leaned out from the driver's seat. She didn't have time to take careful aim. A blast of flames and a ridiculously loud roar issued from the preposterously large muzzle of the weapon, rocking the world. Globes shattered above the two brothers, sending out spray. There wasn't enough time to get off a second shot.

D and the old woman waited silently for the pair of riders approaching in a cloud of dust.

Clay was the first to speak, shouting, "What the hell were those things? We're not even three miles out of town yet!"

Head still drooping, Bingo swayed back and forth on his horse. He was fast asleep, but the fact that he'd raced this far without being thrown made it clear it was no ordinary slumber. Bingo Bullow, after all, was a man who conversed in his sleep.

As Clay gazed up at the unsettling leaden sky, Granny Viper caught his eye. The old woman was bent over in the midst of concealing her blunderbuss.

"Hey! You lousy hag!" Clay shouted at her. As he kept watch over D out of the corner of his eye, he added, "That was a damn fool thing to do. Just look what you did to my hat!" Pulling his cap off, he put one of his fingers into it. His fingertip poked out of a hole near the top—a piece of shot had gone right through it. If he'd been wearing the cap all the way down on his head, it probably would've hit him right in the forehead.

And what did Granny do when met by a look of hatred that would've left a child in tears? She grinned from ear to ear. The smile she wore seemed so amiable, not even the sweetest, kindest woman in the world could've hoped to match it.

"What a piece of luck, eh?" the crone said with sincerity. She then told the astonished Clay, "I wasn't the one who decided to take the shot, though. Our handsome friend here made the call. And I was sure he was likely to cut me down if I didn't do like he said."

That was true enough.

"Is that right?" Clay asked D. In stark contrast to the tone he'd used up until now, his words were soft. He seemed ready to have it out with the Hunter.

And D's reply . . . was no reply at all. "Looks like you didn't get any of their contents on you," the Hunter said, filling his field of view with the two brothers.

Clay gave a knowing nod. "So, that's how it goes, is it? That's your game, then? Well, that's too damn bad. If it was that easy to get the stuff on us, we'd be ashamed to call ourselves the Bullow Brothers."

"The next time they show up, you might not be able to avoid it. Besides, I doubt it would've been life threatening, even if you got some on you."

"And how the hell do you know that?" Clay cried out.

"A hunch," D replied.

"Don't give me any of that shit!"

"Give it a rest," Bingo muttered in a tone as flat and gray as the sky over them. "The Hunter D had a hunch about it. We would've been fine even if we got wet!"

"Spare me. I don't need to hear it from you too, bro."

In a soothing voice, Granny spoke to the frenzied Clay. "Settle down, there. No harm came to you, so everything's okay, isn't it? We'll have no fighting amongst ourselves in this party."

Silence descended. It wasn't a quiet interval for introspection, but rather one brought on by sheer astonishment.

"Who the hell ever said we're in your party?!" Clay shouted, more blood rising to his face.

"Why, you did, the second you left town. We've got the same destination, and we've been traveling less than five hundred yards apart. What's more, it seems our Mr. D has a head full of info on half the nasty critters waiting for us out in the desert."

Holding his tongue for a minute, Clay turned to his older brother and asked, "You think that's true, bro?" His tone was like that of a gullible spectator putting a question to a bogus clairvoyant.

"I don't know," Bingo replied, his head swaying from side to side. "But under the circumstances, traveling together could make things a lot easier later on. And you know what they say: it's the company you keep that really makes the trip."

Eyes that Gleam in the Dark

CHAPTER 2

I

Night soon fell without further incident. After tethering the horses to hooks on the back of the wagon, the whole group settled down for the evening behind a sand dune. A certain air of dignity prevailed over the world. Though darkness had covered everything, the heavens hadn't lost their dull gray clouds, which continued to hang over the heads of the little group. As the temperature fell rapidly, no one said a thing. White breath alone spilled from their lips.

"A hell of a desert this is," Clay groused as he warmed himself by the electronic heater he'd set down in a firmer spot in the sand. "Hot as a bastard by day and cold as a bitch at night. I don't mind it cooling off some, but the damn temperature's dropped more than sixty degrees!"

"There's a good side to it, though," Granny interjected as she held her hands out over Clay's heater.

"Hey, don't be sidling up to my stove like we're best buddies or something. That lousy wagon of yours has a heating system in it, don't it?" the younger Bullow said harshly.

Not the least bit fazed, Granny replied, "That's pretty tight-fisted talk for someone who calls himself a man. Well, with a temperament like that, I'm not surprised you start blubbering at the first little chill. Sure it's cold, but see how the grains of sand get heavier in the lower temperatures so it's not blowing around like it does all day? Of course, it helps there's no wind, either."

"Damn straight," Bingo concurred in a deep voice from a spot some eight or ten feet from Clay. Now the younger Bullow couldn't possibly argue with Granny. But what kind of man could his older brother be? He wasn't by the heater. Why, he wasn't even lying down. He was still astride his cyborg horse, sitting in the kind of hard saddle that ordinarily left a rider numb below the waist after three or more hours of riding.

Granny muttered, "Strange tastes your brother's got." And it came as little surprise that she sounded a bit unnerved.

"Not really. You wanna talk about strange, there's your guy!" Clay said, tossing his jaw in the direction of Granny's wagon.

Leaving his cyborg horse beside the vehicle, D had lain back against a nearby sand dune with his sword in his left hand and his eyes shut.

"If that guy don't look like the loneliest thing ever. And it ain't because he's turned his back on the world. With him, everybody's happy to see him coming, but no one's sorry to see him go. And anybody who catches sight of him is bound to step aside on account of that intense scent he's got about him."

"Yes, the scent," the crone said with a nod as she followed Clay's gaze. "The smell of blood. The scent of solitude. But you still don't get it, do you?"

"Get what?" Clay asked, eyes opening wide.

"She's right," the slender black shadow on horseback said.

"Not you too, bro! You're siding with an old hag over your own brother?"

Before Clay had finished airing his complaint, D sat up without making a sound. Grains of sand spilled like waves down the slope he'd been leaning against. Eyes still closed as he stood up straight, he then froze in place like a bronze sculpture.

"What is it?" Clay asked, squinting his eyes.

Granny's face grew tense, too. There was no trace of movement around them—just the night frozen solid. That's all that was out there.

D's silhouette shifted. With a movement just as brusque as the one that'd put him on his feet in the first place, he seated himself again in the same spot.

Clay and the crone looked at each other.

"What is it?" Clay said again.

The old woman went over to D. "Did something happen?" she asked.

D didn't raise his eyes. "It rained sand," he said.

"Sand?"

"In this desert," the Hunter continued, "what we know about the world doesn't count for much, it seems."

"Did you sense something?"

"It's going to get more dangerous. Try not to make things any worse."

"Is that a fact? Well, we'll be counting on you, in that case," the crone remarked, pursuing the matter no further. If she left things to the Hunter, she couldn't possibly go wrong. Her feelings on the subject were more a matter of rationality than trust—she didn't want to be burdened with too much information when she could have D shouldering it all. Cold air suddenly snaked into her nostrils, and Granny sneezed loudly.

"Hey," Clay called out to D. "You seem to know an awful lot about this desert. So, why don't you tell us what's lying ahead? We're in this together, and we're all headed the same way. Why not share the wealth, eh?" His tone was somewhat belligerent.

D didn't move a muscle.

"Hey, don't play games with me. You plan on keeping everything to yourself?" Clay blustered, not giving up. In a desert crossing such as this, any information about the vicious creatures it contained could literally mean the difference between life and death. He was deadly serious.

"Wait just a second, you two," Granny interrupted. "We've barely finished our first day out here, right? We have a falling out this early in the game, then there's no point in traveling together in the first place. Think about it, D. There's some sense to what he's saying. We don't want to go plodding off across the sands without the slightest clue now. Tell him some of what you know."

"Not some of it. *All* of it." There was composure to the warrior's tone. He was ready to fight if need be. His right hand drifted toward the harp at his waist.

"Come now, D," Granny prodded.

Clay's index finger was poised by his harp. He pulled back on one of the strings, and then he stopped. He saw D open his eyes. Cold water rushed down from the nape of his neck to the base of his spine—the Hunter's glare was that powerful.

"If I tell you, you'll have to go first," D said in the kind of voice that crept along the ground.

"Fine by me," Clay replied with a magnanimous bow. It was no bluff. He seemed to have considerable confidence in himself. "I wouldn't be a weasel and ask you to go first anyhow. I'll plow dead ahead wherever we gotta go. So, just put your mind at ease and tell me all about it."

"The moving forest," said D. Clay noticed that the cloud of white that spilled from the Hunter's lips with his breath was far fainter than that of the rest of them. "If the notes I have are correct, it was about a dozen miles southwest of here. But it *is* a moving forest, after all."

"Meaning there's no telling where it's gone? That's a hoot!"

"The person who left those notes only saw it in motion from a long way off, but didn't go any closer. Whether or not he was lucky in that respect, I can't say."

"I see," said Clay.

"And another thing—there are people."

"What?!" Granny cried, her eyes bugging out. She'd thought whatever else slipped from D's lips couldn't possibly surprise her, but she was wrong. "People out in this desert? Stop pulling my leg."

"That's what it said in the notes," D continued softly. "About thirty in all. Apparently, they attacked on cyborg horses about a hundred and twenty miles south of here. Killed almost a dozen of the traveler's companions and made off with their goods and the corpses."

"What would they take corpses for?" Clay asked.

Giving him no reply, D simply said, "There's more. It seems they were shot and stabbed but did not die."

Silence descended.

Bingo's torso rose from his mount. "Immortal, are they?" he said in a low sleepy voice.

"That's all I know," D said. His eyes were closed.

Clay shrugged his shoulders. "That's no big freaking deal, is it, bro?" he said to the figure on horseback. He sounded thoroughly relieved. Perhaps a desert plagued by beasts and immortal bandits was nothing to them. "That right there scares me a lot more," Clay said, tossing his jaw in the wagon's direction. There was no one but Tae inside, but everyone was well aware of what *the hidden* represented.

It was at just that moment that the wagon's door opened. Clay grimaced awkwardly and rubbed his scruffy beard. Tae's head hung low; it seemed to be something of a habit with the girl. Perhaps averting her gaze had kept the weight of her fate from crushing her.

"Get back inside. It's cold out here," Granny shouted. The rebuff had a touch of animosity to it. While it was her job to find children who'd been "hidden," she was entitled to feel however she liked about her charges.

"Aw, why don't you just leave her be?" Clay said as he glared at the crone's wrinkled face from the corner of his eye. "It's a hell of a lot more comfortable here than blasting the heat in there. Besides, a person's got a right to do whatever they damn well please. She don't have to take orders from anyone. And I'd be tickled pink to have a cutie like her out here instead of all these ugly mugs I'm traveling with."

Knowing as he did Granny Viper's name, Clay also surely had a good idea of the girl's circumstances, but his tone held neither fear nor loathing. No doubt he'd be brimming with confidence until the very moment he died.

Tae quickly ducked back inside.

Giving an appreciative whistle, Clay said, "Now, ain't she a beauty. What's her name, anyway?"

Granny met the man's cheery inquiry with a stern visage. "Let's be perfectly clear on something," she said, her voice rolling across the ground like a toxic cloud. "That girl is my merchandise. Try anything funny and you'll find yourself in hell trying to get some action from a she-devil."

"Well, that'd have to beat looking at your ugly kisser," Clay sneered back. "Your merchandise may be pricey, but that don't mean it's good. We all know what happens to most *hidden* who go back home, so you'd best pray that she ain't one of them."

"You needn't worry about it," Granny replied snidely. "My job just entails getting them home. What happens after that doesn't concern me. On the other hand, until I get 'em there, I'll look out for them even if it costs me my life. And I'm not letting anyone pull anything funny with her."

"Interesting," Clay said, licking his chops. "Well, just let me give you fair warning then. Before this little trip of ours is done, I'm gonna leave my mark on your precious goods."

"Oh, is that right?" Granny shot back, her eyes growing wider by the second.

"Knock it off, Clay," a sober voice said, shattering the tension. It belonged to Bingo. "Well," he continued, "it looks like the best thing to do is pull out of here as soon as possible."

Both Clay and Granny turned in the direction that the skinny figure indicated with a toss of his chin. White sand was dropping all around a form of unearthly beauty. Returning his weapon and sheath to his back, D stared out at one point in the darkness.

"What is it now?" Clay asked with seeming relish.

"Can you make something out?" Bingo inquired sleepily.

"Butterflies," D replied, walking over to his horse without making a sound.

"Hey, Hunter! You just gonna turn tail and run then?" Clay sneered, as if he'd been waiting for the chance to say these exact words.

"So, we've got no choice but to plow right through them?" Bingo added.

Not replying to Bingo's query, D merely said, "I don't think this is a job for me." He was looking right at the old woman.

"So you know what I have up my sleeve, then?" Granny said, her eyes going wide. "If my moves have become public knowledge, I may have to learn a whole new bag of tricks."

Just as D mounted his horse, Granny seated herself in the wagon. With an expression that said he didn't have a clue what was going on, Clay put his feet into the stirrups. Though all of them strained their eyes, they didn't see anything—the darkness drank up every sound, leaving everything in a state of utter silence. D's mount took a few steps away from them.

"Hold up a minute. Won't we be tackling this together?" Granny called out to D.

"I don't remember asking you to follow along after me."

"When you said this wasn't a job for you, was that supposed to mean you're leaving the rest of us to our own devices then? You're not a real compassionate man now, are you?" Granny railed at the Hunter, but D had ridden his horse beyond the reach of her abuse.

Perhaps nothing save the hyper-keen senses of a dhampir could've detected the paper-thin presence that was closing in on them from the depths of the darkness. At long last, the wind moved around them. The flowing air came from the beating of countless wings, yet was still strangely light. The mass consisted of butterflies beyond number—a swarm of thousands, or even tens of thousands. But where did they live, and what did they seek?

They rushed at D, enveloping the tall figure in black with the color of darkness. His blade flashed out. Without so much as the sound of a slash through the air, all of the bisected butterflies started to drop to the ground as D galloped through them. As the mount and rider advanced in a dusty cloud, the wave of black drifted away as if frightened of the Hunter, but an instant later it became a broad band that began following after him. It was only natural that the rest of the swarm set upon the wagon and the other two riders.

"Damnation! What in blazes is this?" Granny screamed from the driver's seat.

"These little buggers sure have some nerve!" Clay shouted as he plucked off a few that were covering his face. The black butterflies relentlessly besieged his livid countenance; Bingo had already been reduced to an ebony sculpture.

Suddenly the world of darkness felt a protest of orange light. Caught in three thousand degrees of flame, the butterflies themselves added fuel to the fire.

Pulling a tank filled with fire-dragon oil and a leather pressure-pump up onto the driver's seat, Granny waved the reinforced plastic nozzle around as she cackled, "Well, how do you like them apples?! Have another taste of one of the Capital's very own flamethrowers. I've still got plenty of this fuel to go around."

And in keeping with the crone's haughty talk, tongues of flame licked out in all directions as helpless butterflies fell like blazing scraps of paper. Not quite so conspicuous due to Granny Viper's furious battle, Clay and Bingo nonetheless were engaging the butterflies about forty feet away. The odd thing was, the butterflies really weren't doing anything. There was no sign of them injecting some solvent to melt the travelers' flesh or clogging their windpipes to suffocate them; they merely kept going after them.

"Damn! No matter how many we fight off, they just keep coming. At this rate, there'll be no end to it, bro."

There was no answer to Clay's remark—Bingo's entire body was draped in black cloth. While the younger Bullow struggled to pull

the insects off his own face, his older brother sat on his horse without moving a muscle. As a result, it looked like he'd grown twice as fat.

"Damn you little pests!" Clay shouted through the airborne butterflies that eclipsed the darkness. And then a beautiful note rang out that sounded like someone strumming a guitar. But what happened when that sound melded with the darkness, and then became a wave that rippled out?

The swarm of butterflies that appeared to float on into eternity all disappeared within a ten-foot radius. Another note resounded: every time the mellifluous sound rang out, the maddening black swarm of insects that rushed in to replace their fallen comrades disappeared. And in the center of the gap that'd opened so suddenly was Clay. His right hand was on the harp he wore on his hip. He kept one eye on his older brother.

"Bingo's fine," the younger Bullow told himself. "The old bag's giving them a hell of a fight, too. Now where the hell's that Hunter gone off to?"

While Granny was indeed on top of the situation, Clay's older brother was blanketed, mount and all, with black butterflies. What was fine about that?

At that very moment, the swarm of butterflies smoothly drifted away. Because the creatures did no harm but merely trailed along after them, Granny and Clay found them all the more disturbing, and their expressions stiffened accordingly.

Gasps of surprise slipped from two pairs of lips at the same time.

The butterflies had begun to glow. So like the darkness in hue, first the contours of their wings and then their entire forms had suddenly begun to take on a silvery light.

"What the hell . . ." Clay muttered as the silver butterflies formed several thick bands before him that then intertwined and began to leisurely eddy about.

This wasn't merely some pattern formed by the capricious flight of the creatures. It was clearly a configuration purposely orchestrated by some higher intelligence. Straight lines and curves, polyhedrons and circles all existed in the same place and time, twisting together and pulling apart again. Yet for all that activity, the swirling figures remained focused on a single point in space.

While they weren't sure how long they'd watched, Granny and Clay felt like they were being pulled into the center of that vortex, and the two of them frantically shut their eyes. A few seconds passed.

"Looks like it's over," said a cold voice that sounded equidistant from the pair as it set their eardrums trembling. Opening their eyes in unison, they found a man on horseback stopped about fifteen feet from them. It was D.

"I just knew you'd be back," Granny exclaimed with joy, still holding a nozzle that dripped liquefied fat.

"Looks like he came back once he found out the butterflies were harmless," Clay muttered scornfully.

"I just came to tell you something," D said dispassionately from the back of his horse.

"Oh? And what would that be?"

"A tornado has sprung up nearly a mile ahead of us. Not a very large one, but enough to pick all of us up. It'll be here in about five minutes."

Of course, Granny and Clay must've wanted to know how the young Hunter had eluded the swarm of butterflies, and whether or not he'd watched their dizzying display until the end, but the threat of natural disaster took precedence over all else. As she stowed the flamethrower again, Granny asked the young man apprehensively, "You'll be going with us, won't you?"

Needless to say, his reply was the same as always: "You're free to follow me if you like."

II

While a pale ash colored the east, light began to rain down at the same rate the darkness dissipated. It was dawn.

The group had moved about three miles west from their first encampment and was sheltered behind a sand dune. When the wagon door opened quietly, a pale and reserved-looking face peered out. Roaring snores crept from the vehicle's interior—the whole group had gone to bed about three hours earlier. Tae looked around sleepily at her surroundings, but they weren't particularly terrifying. Behind a dune to her right lay a lumpy blanket where the toes of a pair of boots jutted from the end. Apparently, that was Clay. There was no sign of his older brother, and his horse wasn't with Clay's, either. There was no telling where a man like that could've gone. Sweeping another seventy degrees, Tae's eyes then halted. A figure in black was reflected in her widened pupils.

D was on the crest of a dune, staring off to the west. His form was reminiscent of the most exquisite sculpture, and as he focused solely on the direction they were headed, he had an air of intensity about him that suited the situation perfectly.

Tae climbed down from the wagon and headed for the dune. For a girl who seemed to have lost her own will and who was manipulated like a doll by the old woman, this was an unbelievably purposeful course of action. Climbing the dune, she was a few yards from the Hunter when she came to a halt. It was the words that came over the back of his black coat that stopped her.

"What brings you out here?" he asked.

Tae didn't answer.

"There's no telling what'll come at us next out in this desert. Go back to the wagon." His voice was soft, but it allowed no debate.

Tae closed her eyes. Her head still hung low, and her thin, bloodless lips trembled with fright. "I . . . I thought I might . . . answer your question . . ."

Back at the cheap hotel, D had asked the girl the name of the Noble who'd abducted her. Now it was a different question he put to her. "Do you want to tell me?" he asked.

Tae looked up at D with an expression that betrayed her surprise.

"Why have you decided to talk about it? If you don't want to, don't force yourself to do it."

The girl didn't know what to say.

"Did Granny put you up to this?"

Tae looked down again. It took a few seconds before she could speak again. "If you didn't feel like helping . . . she said none of us would make it across the desert alive . . . that's why . . ."

"Your parents are in Barnabas, aren't they?"

Several more seconds of silence followed.

"It seems both of them are dead," the girl replied. "But my big brother got married and took over the house."

"In that case, you needn't burden yourself unduly for the rest of the trip. I can't take you there, but you're free to follow me."

Tae looked at D strangely. The black expanse of his back spoke volumes on loneliness and complete isolation. Somehow, she got the impression that the young man had nothing more to say to her. Tae backed away a few steps; she was too afraid to just turn around. Right as she was about to go, the girl hesitantly said, "I don't remember anything at all. Just . . ."

Just what?

"In the darkness, there were always these two red eyes, blazing like rubies . . . watching me . . ."

The Hunter hadn't turned toward her, and the girl then turned her back to him, too.

Not long after the sloping dune had hidden the tracks she left in the sand, another voice—a hoarse one—could be heard where D seemed to be alone. "Well, it looks like *he* got a taste of her after all," it said with a chuckle. "In which case she'll never know happiness no matter how she might try, eh? So, what do you suppose he did to her?"

There was no reply. D just kept his eyes trained straight ahead at the cold world of sand that seemed shrouded in gray light.

The voice laughed with amusement. "She may be behaving herself right now, but he isn't crazy enough to snatch a human girl just so she can be his maidservant. Sooner or later, that girl's bound to show her true colors. Our foes aren't on the outside, but rather—"

"There are some girls that nothing happens to," D finally replied.

"Sure, but that's maybe one in ten thousand," the voice shot back ruthlessly. "And just think about the miserable end this world has in store for all the rest of those girls—and I don't just mean the ones *he* took."

If that comment had been directed at anyone but D, they would've grown pale as they tried desperately to strike the answer from their brain, or perhaps they would've frozen on the spot from the overwhelming horror of it.

For *the hidden*, the tragedy really began when they were found and brought back to the world of humanity. There were girls who might suddenly sprout fangs and tear into someone's throat the very day they were reunited with their parents. There were boys who might live uneventfully for months, or even years, before going mad without any warning whatsoever. There were actually records of a case a dozen years or so earlier where such children abandoned their parents again to live someplace in the mountains, but even there the madness in their blood set them to killing each other, until in the end they were all dead. You could say both the beginning and the end of *the hidden*'s tragic tale was penned when the children disappeared.

"You know how it is," D's left hand continued. "In the end, nothing good can come of that girl going back to her family. At first, her parents will weep for joy. They'll probably want her to live with them, even if it means hiding her from the neighbors or moving to another region. But after a while, they'll get to wondering if maybe her eyes don't have a strange glint to them. Not that you can blame them. To eyes that have peered into the darkness of the other side, this world is a hollow reflection. And could anything shy of the sights of hell ever move those kids again? No, not till the end of time. And there's the first act of the tragedy. The very parents who would've died to have their kid back now can't even look at them. They lock the kid in their room. And then one day the two of them pack up a wagon and take off out of the blue, leaving just their kid in the house."

The voice broke off there; D was squeezing his left hand into a fist. He did so with such force it wouldn't have been surprising to hear the bones cracking.

But from his fist, a tortured voice said, "I suppose you could say the kids that get left behind are the lucky ones, though. Some parents are more . . . *thorough*. The same parents who spent their last dalas searching for their kids one day start whittling down a piece of wood and putting a point on the end of it . . ."

Something red had slowly begun to seep from between D's fingers.

"Oof . . . No one can really say . . . who it's harder for . . . the parents or the kids . . . But I can tell you this . . . If that girl there never goes home . . . no one . . . gets . . . hurt . . ."

At that moment, D quietly turned around. Seemingly following Tae's tracks, he went down the dune. After mounting his cyborg horse, he wheeled around in the direction of Clay and the wagon.

"There's a tornado approaching," the Hunter declared. "We're moving out."

After just enough time to contemplate his words, the blanket rose and the door to the wagon opened. Both the old woman and the warrior had been awake for some time. They certainly weren't average travelers.

"What, again?" Clay complained.

"Seriously?" Granny Viper asked, just to be sure. "I mean, it's not like that sort of thing springs up all the time. So, I take it this is a different one from last night, right?"

"No, it's the same one," D said flatly.

"Meaning all of *what*, exactly?" Clay asked, his lascivious expression twisting into a sneer. "Are you trying to tell us ol' Mr. Twister's out looking for us or something?"

Ignoring him, D started riding to the east.

"Son of a bitch," Clay growled, hatred in his eyes, as he hustled after the Hunter and toward his own horse.

Granny made haste, too.

No sooner had the wagon taken off than Clay did something rather strange. Looking all around, he cupped one hand by his mouth and shouted as loudly as he could, "Bro, I'm going on ahead. You catch up with me later, okay?"

Though Bingo didn't seem to be anywhere within range of Clay's cries, it seemed like his younger brother might have been able to see him. Saying nothing more and not seeming at all anxious, the warrior lashed his horse into action. As he galloped toward the wagon that was already twenty or thirty yards ahead of him, he looked over his shoulder.

"God, that's unbelievable," Clay said, the words spilling from him like a trickle of disbelief.

Distance-wise, it must've still been a couple of miles away—a line that looked like a twisted metal wire tied the heavens to the earth. It was bizarre the way that either end was blurred, seemingly dissolving into the sky at one extreme and the ground at the other. As far as Clay could see, it just kept growing thicker and thicker.

Riding full-tilt, the younger Bullow pulled even with the wagon. Granny Viper also wore a look of desperation as she gripped the reins. She recognized the tornado for what it was now.

The door opened, and Tae's face appeared.

"Don't come out here," Clay barked, but it was the old woman's expression, instead, that stiffened at the remark. Tae remained as devoid of emotion as ever.

Clay rode up on D's right-hand side. For a split second the desire to take a shot at the Hunter from behind surfaced in his brain, but it quickly faded again. "What the hell's the story with this tornado?!" he shouted. "It's following us! A while back, I joked it was looking for us, but this is just—"

"It's a strange desert, isn't it?" D said in a rare response.

"Damned if I ever heard of a tornado chasing travelers all night long. But we managed to give it the slip once already. We'll just do it again, right?"

Giving no reply, D flicked his gaze to the rear.

Imitating him, Clay looked back as well…and groaned despite himself.

The tornado looked like it was three feet thick now instead of a thin wire. The distance was dwindling; it wasn't a mile away now, or even five hundred yards.

Shouting something, Clay kicked his horse's flanks. As he shot away from D, he heard the Hunter behind him say, "The wagon's going to be sucked in." His voice was cold, like a machine's. Clay quivered, as if an electrical current had just shot through his powerful back.

"Do something, D!" Granny cried, her voice trailing after the Hunter.

Grains of sand buffeted all of their faces.

"This seriously ain't good," Clay muttered as he pulled back on the reins. Letting D pass him, he pulled up next to the wagon. "Granny, send the girl over here," he shouted. His eyes were glittering.

"Don't make me laugh! Why, I'd no sooner trust a goddamn rapist like you than—"

"I'm a lot faster than your wagon. We might just be able to get away."

"Give it a rest. Before I'd ever give her to you, I'd let the whirlwind have her."

"If that's the way you want it."

Clay flew into the air. His huge form seemed to become feather-light, and he landed right next to the old woman. He then bulled his way to the door.

"Stop it. If you don't, I'll—"

Powerful winds tore away the rest of Granny's cry. Not only did it tug at her words, but her body as well—the instant the edge of the fiercely writhing, sand-lifting pillar of black touched the wagon, both the vehicle and its three passengers were thrown high into the sky.

III

As Tae's consciousness pulled away from the darkness, the conviction that she had returned to reality hit her. She was lying down. Beneath her, it was soft. Sand, no doubt. And it was hot. The sand was scorching. Slowly, Tae moved her limbs. She wasn't in great pain. The dull throbbing she felt here and there was from being tossed around inside the wagon when it was picked up by the tornado. Propping herself up with both arms, she looked all around. A sense of incongruity dug into her spine.

The endless expanse of sand was gone; right before her towered a fairly high mound of stone. It looked about a hundred and fifty feet high. Come to mention it, she was surrounded on all sides by rocks large and small. As it occurred to her that it wouldn't be that strange to find such a rock formation in the desert, Tae picked herself up off the ground. Sweat spread across the back of her neck. She had no idea what time it was.

"Well, little lady, looks like you made it okay," someone called from the rock behind her, prompting her to turn in a daze. When she did, her eyes caught the massive form of a man in a brimless blue cap. Feeling the malicious lust in his eyes as he watched her, Tae backed away a few steps.

"Don't go being so cold with me, now," Clay said, a broad smile creeping across his face as he approached her. The beads of sweat covering his face glistened. "I just came to a minute ago myself. This is a hell of a place to find ourselves. Could be me and you are the only two who survived, you know. In which case, it'd be better for both of us if we could play nice, now wouldn't it?"

"Keep away from me."

"Well, now. You got a lot more to say than I thought, don't you? I didn't really get to hear what you were jawing about with the

Vampire Hunter. But I'd sure like to hear me some of that sexy voice of yours."

Before Clay had finished speaking, he pulled the girl's tiny body close to his own massive form. Given almost no time to resist, Tae was pushed back against the sand.

"Stop it!" Tae screamed as fingers hard as rock sank into her breasts through her blouse. When she tried to push the warrior off, her hands were caught by the wrist and twisted up over "her head. Clay's lips came closer. The girl desperately turned her face away. His lips touched her cheek. Suddenly all the strength drained from the girl, and Clay knit his brow. Regardless, he sought her lips again. She was as unresponsive as a wax effigy.

"What the hell?! You giving in already? That's no fun at all. C'mon. Scream or cry or something!"

Though the younger Bullow believed his words had carried sufficient threat, Tae's expression hadn't changed at all. This wasn't just some trick to rob him of his carnal urges.

Unable to stand it any longer, Clay shouted, "Hey!" and shook the girl by the shoulders. Taking her chin in hand, he turned her face back. The instant their eyes met, a moan slipped from him. What occupied Tae's eyes was something humans were never meant to see. Sadness and hatred, suffering and fear—all of those emotions commingled in her eyes, but more than anything they were shrouded with a distant coldness beyond imagining.

"You felt that all those years . . ." Clay muttered absentmindedly.

"I remember . . . a little . . ." the eighteen-year-old girl said in a tone that could freeze even a hardened fighting man. "A little of what happened to me there . . . You're exactly the same . . . All of you . . . Humans and *them* . . ."

"You mean you were . . ." Clay muttered, and then a harsh sound rang out. With a cry like a wild animal he pulled back, and then sprang forward. A howl through the wind followed after him: a mighty lash from a leathery whip.

"Prepare to take your medicine. I'll flay the hide off your hands and face!" Granny shouted from beside a massive boulder five or ten feet to the right of where Clay had first appeared. The whip whistled; it hardly seemed possible that an old woman was manipulating the whip as it dealt Clay a blow that stung to the bone.

Eyes still shielded by both hands, he hurled a single insult: "You fucking hag!" Once again, Clay leapt back, and a beautiful sound rang through the air. A split second later, half of the whip that was snaking after the man's massive form disappeared like a puff of smoke. At a loss for words, Granny stiffened with tension.

"I'm gonna punch your ticket, you old bag!" Clay shouted, his right hand creeping across his harp. A prismatic cloud suddenly spread before his eyes.

It was sand. The very instant that she saw Clay was drawing on his own skill, Granny quickly discarded her whip and pulled the sand from the jar at her waist. However, the strange color of the sand and the way she used it made it clear that this was no simple trick to blind her opponent.

The sand that fell between the crone's feet and the tips of Clay's boots began to take human form—an image of Clay himself appeared on the ground.

Something gleamed in the old woman's right hand. The moment the short knife she kept hidden on her stabbed into the sand painting on the ground, Clay clutched his right ear with one hand. Redness seeped out between the palm of his hand and his cheek, but he didn't make a sound.

"What do you want carved up next? An eye, or maybe your nose?"

Buffeted with the kind of threats that made grown men and fire dragons alike freeze in their tracks, Clay smirked as if the situation was so amusing that he just couldn't help himself. "Granny Viper, People Finder—I guess the name ain't just for show after all," he said. "*Now* things are starting to get good. This is just the way I like it!"

"I was about to say the same thing myself," Granny said, licking her lips. The situation was rapidly escalating to a dangerous boiling point where more blood could be spilt and lives could be lost.

And then someone said, "Hold it right there."

Both of them froze at that pitch-black voice. Two pairs of eyes zipped halfway up the rocky mound, where the hem of a black long coat billowed out in the scant breeze. It wasn't clear whether it was Granny or Clay who mumbled D's name.

"Put your personal differences aside until we figure out what's going on with the desert. Where's the girl?" the Hunter asked.

Clay and Granny finally noticed that Tae was no longer there. An almost pitiful look of distress rose on the old woman's haughty countenance.

Tae came around the rocks and wiped her lips. Bewilderment and despair were rising from the pit of her stomach, spreading through her whole body. She didn't know what she was going to do next, or even what she should do. She started walking. She didn't want to sit there crying, though she wasn't really sure why she shouldn't. She wasn't sure where she was going; all she knew was that wanted to get away from everyone.

As countless phantoms flickered in her consciousness, one vivid image came to the fore, and then faded: crimson eyes glowing in the darkness . . . coming closer.

Where will I go? What will I do?

Those eyes were peering into her patiently. As she tried to squeeze out a scream, her throat convulsed, barely choking it off. From behind the crimson glow, a pale visage vaguely drifted into view. It was a face that was incredibly beautiful, manly, and above all, sad. An emotion that felt like crystal-clear water filled the girl's heart.

Compared to that, she thought, *compared to the fate that fashioned those eyes and that face, my pain is nothing.*

The red points of light faded.

Tae noticed she'd come to a standstill. *I should go back,* she thought. Though she had no idea what awaited her, she decided to forge ahead anyway. Then suddenly Tae turned right back around as she heard something stir behind her. She looked over her shoulder. A good two seconds passed before she could push a scream past her lips.

The first one to race over to the girl was Clay. The instant he came around the rocks, he saw Tae running toward him. Steadying the girl who'd just thrown herself at his chest, he then concentrated his gaze on the person before him. It was a man clad in a tattered shirt and trousers. Covered with a bushy overgrowth of hair and beard, his face looked emaciated, although his physique was relatively well-defined. The man stood there dazed for a few seconds and then fell to his knees on the spot.

"What in blazes do we have here?" Granny said from behind Clay.

"I don't know. By the look of him, he seems like a traveler lost in the desert. But how the hell could he get by living in this hole in the rocks? Could be dangerous."

Grabbing Tae by the arm and pulling her away, Granny told the warrior, "You'll have to help me while I bring her away someplace safe. If you're a real man, you'll take care of matters here." And then she beat a hasty retreat.

"Who the hell are you?" Clay asked, his fingers still poised on his harp. Murderous intent billowed from every inch of his body—it would've been enough to make the average person collapse on the spot. He was head-and-shoulders above the warriors and Hunters found everywhere else.

Scared perhaps by the younger Bullow's demeanor, the man shook his head repeatedly and raised both hands defenselessly. "How . . . how did all of you get here?" he asked. It almost sounded like his windpipe was clogged with sand.

Odd as it was, it prompted Clay to reply, "We got scooped up by a mean old tornado and went for a little flight."

Clay watched with surprise as the other man's shoulders slumped part-way through his reply. His hands came down to hide his face. "It got you, too? I just knew it. We'll all be stuck here for the rest of our lives . . ."

"What's that?!" Clay bellowed. "Just what do you mean by that? And who the hell are you, anyway?!"

When Clay took a step toward the other man, his eyes were drawn to several riders coming around the base of the mountain. Perhaps noticing them too, the man who'd been crouched there suddenly leapt back up, gave a frightened cry, and raced over to Clay. Just as the ragged man was about to collide with him, Clay dodged easily to the right and stuck his foot out. Falling forward with great impetus, the man threw a cloud of dust high into the air. But he quickly got back up again. He might have clutched at Clay's legs, but the warrior effortlessly backed away to keep the contact from happening.

"Please, help me," the man groaned. "I ran away from them. Up until yesterday, I was one of them. There was no use trying to escape . . . no one's getting out of this damn desert!" the man cried with the most appalling look of hopelessness hammered into his worn face.

But Clay did him one better as he glared back at the stranger with an almost demonic expression. "Don't make me laugh, you little coward. Unless you want me to turn you over to them, you'd best promise to answer me straight about everything I wanna know. If you do, I'll chase 'em off for you. If not, I'll personally see to it that they butcher you on the spot."

"Okay," the man said, nodding without complaint. Although his face didn't look like that of a weak-willed person, the man exhibited considerable fear.

"Just so long as we're clear on that. Wait behind me, then. Oh, and one more thing: you gotta promise me you'll keep your mitts off the girl."

"Whatever you say."

"Good. Get back there. You can relax now." As he listened to the man scurrying behind him for cover, Clay stood there waiting for the approaching dust cloud.

Though the man said that these were his compatriots, there must've been a grave mistake. Astride cyborg horses that looked brand new, the group of men wore shirts so neat and starched they looked freshly laundered. There were four of them.

"Hey there!" Clay called out, raising his left hand in greeting. The gazes that met him were like stone. His smile never fading a bit, the warrior continued, "We went and got ourselves carried off by a tornado. We're in a spot of trouble, seeing as we don't know where we're at now. So, this is great. You guys sure are a sight for sore eyes. Just whereabouts would this happen to be?"

"We came for the man," said the middle-aged man who stood at the fore—a powerfully built character, who seemed to be their leader. His voice was impenetrable. It was devoid of every emotion a human—or any creature, for that matter—normally possessed. Actually, the voice would've sounded more natural coming from a rock. "You're coming with us, too."

Clay bared his teeth in a pearly smile. "That's fine by me. I had me a good upbringing, and I ain't too tough. See, I hate to go anywhere alone. But this other guy says he don't wanna go back, so I don't reckon there's any way to satisfy everybody here."

The men didn't even exchange glances with one another.

"Is that a fact?" the leader said. "In that case . . ."

Seeing the middle-aged man's hand go for the firearm in his belt, Clay swung his right hand up from below. The broadsword he'd hidden up his sleeve became a flash of white that pierced the man's throat. The man's hand was on his gun; Clay saw the muzzle of it turn toward his chest. It disgorged flame. The breechblock moved back, and a sleek empty cartridge flew from the weapon.

Taking a hit from an explosive round that could've easily blown a human head apart on impact, Clay just smiled. The inner lining of his shirt came from the bark of the armor oak, which was harder than rock. His right hand flowed across the strings of his harp releasing a tremendous sound.

The man at the fore of the group became an ash-gray statue, and an instant later the same fate befell his horse. They both fell to the ground in a dusty cloud. There would be no further attacks; the three others behind the leader had turned to dust, too. Perhaps the only reason one rider and mount at the very back still retained their original shape in this sandy form was because they were at the very end of the audibility range for the sound.

"Maybe they don't die, but they seem to turn to dust just fine," Clay said as he raised his right hand and hacked off one of the motionless horse's legs. Not bothering to watch the new pile of sand the collapsing figures created, Clay looked up. He had no idea where they'd been hiding, but another horse and rider now galloped away about fifty yards from him. "Son of a bitch!" he moaned, cursing his own carelessness.

Taking his harp in hand, he turned it toward the rider fleeing over a rise. The device generated ultrasonic waves that destroyed the molecular structure of any material, and as if to compensate for the cruelty of those sound waves, the vibrating strings also created splendid melodies.

However, Clay didn't have a chance to unleash another deadly attack with his fingers. The one surviving attacker suddenly saw a figure standing in the road before him. His horse didn't stop. The moment it looked like the beast's iron-shod hooves were going to trample him, the shadowy figure leapt up. Even after D landed, with his long coat spread out around him, the horse and rider kept right on running. But when the longsword clicked smoothly back into the sheath on D's back, the rider's head finally left his shoulders and rolled across the road.

"Glad you could pitch in at the end there," Clay said as sarcastically as possible to D, who walked toward him without even glancing at the results his own skill had wrought. "Where the hell did you run off to after you found out the girl was missing? Weren't trying to get a preview of my skills, were you? No, you wouldn't do any petty shit like that. Went to check out the neighborhood, right? You're a cold customer. Didn't you give any thought to what'd happen if I found the girl? And you left me to handle all of them, too. If I got killed, the old bag and girl would've both been goners, you know."

"You didn't get killed," was all D said.

Clay had no reply, and that was the end of it. But three pairs of frightened eyes greeted the approaching beauty in black.

The Living Desert

CHAPTER 3

I

The man said his name was Lance and that he was part of a farm group improving crops in the northern Frontier. The group had developed a new strain that would bear fruit even in cold areas without water; they'd selected this desert to stage their experiments some five years earlier. Traveling in a caravan of five trailers bearing a hundred thousand seedlings, the farmers fell victim to a sandstorm and were attacked by a pack of bandits. Regardless of whether they offered any resistance or not, all were slain. Lance himself had been hit, but for some reason the bandits pulled out the gun they'd shoved in his mouth and brought him back to their hideout. The reason Lance went along with all of this was because, in the heat of battle, he'd seen that no matter how many times the bullets and blades of his compatriots had found their mark, the bandits had been utterly unfazed—and he valued his own life. As soon as they arrived back at the bandits' lair, however, Lance realized he'd been drawn into a world beyond imagining.

"You see, the first thing they did was tell me their age. The leader said he was going to turn two hundred that year. And the other bandits did the same, saying they were a hundred, or a hundred and fifty, or whatever the hell they felt like. I laughed at them—at least I had enough backbone left for that. It's what they showed me next that tore the very soul out of me."

"And what was that?" Granny asked eagerly.

"Their stomachs. One by one they took off their shirts. And then . . ."

Lance pressed both hands over his face. They were in a cave they'd found in a rocky mound. The air was sultry, but it was better than being outside. Luckily, they also found Granny's wagon intact, so for the time being they were set as far as food and weapons went.

"What did you see?" Granny asked, growing pale as she did so.

"They were mummies, you see." Under the fresh new shirt of every last one of them, the stomach-wrenching remains of desiccated flesh clung to their bones. "Yet they were perfectly normal from the neck up—as you saw earlier. They turned their ordinary faces at me and grinned. I tell you, I thought I was done for then and there."

The mandate Lance got from them was strange and cruel; he was to work alongside these living corpses as they carried out their mission of slaughtering any travelers who ventured into the desert. How could Lance refuse them?

"In the past five years, we've attacked four parties," Lance said. "I killed folks, too. Men, women—people I didn't know at all. If I didn't do it, they would have killed me. One of them was a girl about your age, too, Miss. Now, I won't tell you I was out of my mind when I did it. I puked my guts up every time I did someone in. But that didn't mean I was happy with the way things were going, either. When I heard you'd been brought here, I decided I'd get away for sure this time no matter what happened to me."

"You said we were brought here. What do you mean by that?" Clay asked as his eyes moved to the cave's entrance.

D was leaning against the rock wall. At that distance, it was difficult to tell whether or not the Hunter could overhear the group's conversation. As he'd helped cut down Lance's pursuers, one would think he'd be quite interested in this discussion, but he didn't ask a single question or even move from where he stood. Ordinary expectations couldn't begin to apply to the Hunter.

"So, who the hell controls the tornado? You've been living out here for five years. You gotta at least know that much. And those freaking mummies gotta be working for the same person, right?"

"No doubt," Lance replied, nodding feebly. "But I can't even begin to guess who—or what—might be behind all this. All those years I watched them carefully, hoping to get some clue as to who it was, but I don't even know if it was someone human or not. Something tells me they don't work for any mortal."

The reason Lance believed this was because of the way he'd been kept alive. His sustenance had consisted of one meal a day of some unknown leaves and berries that were left piled unceremoniously in front of his quarters. Though he tried, he was never able to see who placed the meal there. Lance's meals usually were brought to him while he slept. If he stayed awake to keep watch, nothing would come. After a few weeks, a strange sensation came over Lance. No matter where he was, he had the feeling he was being watched constantly. Even out in the barren desert without another creature around, the feeling remained with him. Of course, escape was impossible. When they weren't attacking travelers, the mummies lay in their cave. Any getaway plans Lance might've come up with were always foiled by sandstorms—or something even stranger.

"And what the hell was *that*?" Clay asked.

Lance merely shook his head at the question. "I don't know. Well, I'd heard about it, but I'd never seen it before. It was water that just stretched on forever. I guess it must've been that 'sea' thing folks talk about."

Clay and Granny exchanged glances.

The Nobility's transportation system was still operational in the Capital, but the further away from the city one went, the worse traveling conditions got. Aside from a few exceptions, people had only the most primitive means of transportation to rely on almost everywhere on the Frontier. Not only did most people live their entire lives without ever seeing the sea, but many died without ever setting foot outside their own village.

Lance's words were sufficient enough to amaze both Clay and Granny.

"There's no sea in the desert," the old woman groaned. "It might've been a spell, or something set up by the Nobility, I guess. What do you think?" Her query was aimed at D.

Lying down in a hollow about ten feet from the rest of the group, Tae turned her eyes toward the Vampire Hunter for the first time.

"The tornado is under someone's control," D said, his eyes still trained on the vista before him. "Whoever controls it brought all of us here. There can only be one reason for that—to have us do the same thing it made him do, I suppose."

"What, you mean plundering?" Clay blurted out without the slightest reserve. "But nobody's loony enough to try crossing this desert anymore. No one other than this old bag, my brother, and me, that is. Anyway, we haven't been attacked by the freaking mummies. What's that supposed to mean?"

"That the desert has some purpose other than killing us, and so it lets us live," D replied plainly. "The man said he was being watched. Now, it's our turn for the same."

"Wait just a minute there!" Granny interrupted. "Just now, you said something about what the desert wants. What's the story? You mean to tell me everything that's attacked us so far is following orders from the *desert*?"

"It shouldn't come as a surprise. I told you about the moving forest. And I suppose you know about the living mountain in the northwestern sectors of the Frontier."

"Sure," Granny said, shivering at the thought of fifty billion tons of rock moving along the horizon. "But that's just a simple mineral-based life form that can't do anything aside from move. Of course, it only occurs maybe once in a decade, but then again, thousands of people get crushed when it does."

"It wouldn't be that unusual for a more complex creature to exist," D said, though it hardly sounded like a rebuttal. "Because the metabolism of mineral-based life forms is greatly restricted by their weight, they really can't hope to develop any further. But the same might not be true for the desert."

"You keep talking about this desert, but I just don't get it. You mean to say—"

"It could be a living creature with a developed nervous system and circuits for thought. But even I can't say exactly what either of those would be like."

"Okay, let me see if I've got this right. You're saying that the tornado was some kind of 'hand' that brings what the desert needs here? That it had 'eyes' that watched this guy? Just where are the nose and mouth then? Oh, I suppose you're gonna tell me those were the globes and butterflies we ran into at the start?"

D didn't respond.

"See, I've got another theory," Clay said, brushing off the dirt as he stood up. He'd been kneeling there listening to what Granny said. "For the time being, let's just forget why this character might've been brought here. But the reason other travelers were robbed and killed is pretty obvious. It's because whoever's pulling the strings is greedy, of course! And so far as I know, there ain't nobody with that kind of greed—nobody but humans."

"You know, you just might have a point there," the old woman said matter-of-factly.

But it was Lance himself that refuted the younger Bullow. "If you turn south from here," the man said, "there's a huge depression in the ground. Everything we stole is sitting in it, rotting or rusting."

Granny and Clay exchanged glances.

"You mean to say someone just chucked it all?" the warrior asked incredulously.

"I really can't say, as I never actually saw it being thrown away. But every last thing we took went off to the dump after about a week."

"So, what did they do with the goods while they had them then?"

Lance just shrugged at the old woman's query.

"At any rate, the first thing we gotta do is get the hell out of this hole in the wall," Clay said, looking around at his companions. "Hey, old lady—get in your wagon. We're getting out of here."

"It's no use," Lance said in a weary tone. "Hell, I tried a hundred times myself. But sometimes there'd be sandstorms, other times it was mirages of the sea. Oh, yeah—there were times I'd walk out and nothing at all would happen and I'd think to myself I was in the clear. And then there'd be this big damn mountain towering right in front of me."

"Well, this time it's gonna work just fine," Clay spat back. In his eyes, Lance must've been nothing more than a coward. "I hate to break it to you, but if we don't get out of here, you ain't either. According to what 'pretty boy' says, it seems we were brought here to take your place. Meaning, whoever controls this here desert don't have any further use for you."

A look of incomparable horror shot across Lance's face.

"Those creeps didn't come here to take you back earlier—I bet they came to kill you. Hell, we can leave you here and let them finish you off, if you like." Watching with relish as Lance's shoulders drooped, Clay then turned to D and said, "You're coming, too, right?"

"It's no use."

Realizing that the Hunter's frosty response was exactly the same as Lance's, Clay got a gleam of light in his eyes—a vicious spark. "What do you mean it's no use?"

"Is your wagon still in one piece, Granny?" D asked.

"Yeah, she'll move somehow or other. Horses are fine, too. But I don't think either could go through that again."

"If we get picked up by another tornado, her wagon will be ruined. Then we'll be out of luck."

"Well, what do you suggest we do, then?" Clay asked, suddenly kicking at the ground. A few small stones vanished into the dark reaches of the cave. "Are we just gonna sit here with our thumbs up our asses? You planning on staying here for the rest our lives, eating nuts and berries like this chump?"

"Do whatever you like," D said, pulling away from the rock wall. It was probably his way of saying he'd handle things his own way. Silently, he moved to the cavern's entrance.

"Is something coming?" Granny asked, squinting her eyes.

"Horses. Ten or so, with riders. His compatriots, no doubt."

"Came to shut him up, did they?" Granny replied, putting her right hand on her jar. "Hell, if there's only a dozen or so, I can take care of 'em one-handed," Granny quipped, but her words met only the empty space where D had been.

"D," Tae mumbled softly.

II

D stepped out into the light, although it was really only light in comparison to the cave. The sky, as always, was shrouded in clouds. At the entrance to the cave, the Hunter looked up at the sky. It was dim—so dim that it merely served to make D's gorgeous countenance seem all the more radiant. He stood quietly, without moving. It was as if he was looking at something beyond the lead-gray sky. But what? Glistening green plains or bright tropical lands would surely mean nothing more to this young man than an arrangement of air and land and colors. What of life, then? Or death? Or fate? Darker than dark and colder than cold, his crystal-clear eyes reflected nothing save the dusty cloud that had twisted around the rocky crag.

There were ten riders. They were the living dead, and a fair bit cleaner than Lance. Surely they'd come here because their earlier colleagues had failed to return. They didn't look at the faces of the four men that Clay and D had dispatched. It appeared the false life the desert had given them once couldn't be theirs a second time.

The living dead formed a semi-circle in front of D. A man with a mustache took a half-step forward. For all intents and purposes, he appeared human. "You're all going to be staying," he said in an almost mechanical voice. A gunpowder pistol hung at his waist. The rounds it could hurl from its six tiny chambers would go right through a tree trunk. "If you give us the man, you have our guarantee you'll be allowed to live here. You'd be wise to take us up on that," the man said flatly, and then he waited.

There was no reply. He was dealing with D, after all.

"Then I guess we can't avoid this, can we?" the man with the mustache said, raising his right hand.

The air was filled with the sounds of gears meshing. All the men on horseback had cocked their guns.

"You, in particular, interest us greatly," he told the Hunter. "If at all possible, we'd like to avoid a confrontation."

Wind buffeted the man's cheeks. And then laughter did the same. Not from D—that young man didn't even know how to laugh. The voice came from the Hunter's left hand, which he'd lowered naturally.

A dangerous silence came over the world.

The mustached man's hand went for the grip of his gun. That was the signal. The row of men pulled their triggers. Or rather, they tried to. But a cloud of yellow sand spread before them like a wall.

Weapons roared. There was the sound of the combustible gas in one tiny metal cylinder after another propelling wads of lead from the weapons' barrels. Orange sparks flashed somewhere in the sandy cloud, and between them streaked a silvery gleam. What happened within that cloud of sand was anyone's guess.

The billowing curtain of sand suddenly dropped to the ground. And with it fell the horsemen. Only D remained standing.

All of the other men had their heads split open and had turned to ash, but D didn't even look at them as he walked over to the only one of them who appeared to have fallen to the ground unscathed—the man with the mustache. The blade the Hunter thrust smoothly under the man's nose was not only free of blood, but of the faintest speck of dust as well.

"The dead should stay that way," D said softly. "How do we get out of this place?"

"I don't know," the man replied, shaking his head. He was pale. His lack of color seemed to spring not so much from fear as from pain. With utter loathing, he added, "And I hope you all wind up like me. Used for the rest of your life by this desert—whatever the hell it really is—and brought back again when you're dead . . . That'd be just perfect," the bandit laughed.

There was a smooth *clink*! D had just sheathed his longsword. At the same time, the man's torso slipped off to the left. Sliced from the right armpit to the left hip, his body turned to dust and vanished before the two pieces could fully separate.

"This is a fine mess you've made," D's left hand chortled. "I don't think that Lance character knows the way out, either." Surely not even the mummies could've imagined the curtain of sand that'd issued from that very same mouth.

"And do you know?"

"More or less. But I haven't been fed enough to know an exact direction when one might not even exist."

D turned right around. Four people stood at the entrance to the cave. Even Clay couldn't hide the surprise that colored his ferocious countenance.

"Ten of them . . . and in less than two seconds. You're a goddamn monster . . ." the younger Bullow fairly groaned. "I wanna kill you more than ever now. With my own two hands."

"I'll thank you to hold off on that until we're across this desert," Granny said in a strident tone. Turning to Lance, she said, "Well, that takes care of the mob that was after you. Now, relax and see if you can't remember something better to tell us, okay? I'll be damned if I'm gonna hang around here playing bandit."

Putting his hand to the brim of his hat, D looked over his shoulder. "Escape is possible," he said.

"What?" more than one person exclaimed as they opened their eyes wide with amazement.

"But as long as we're out in the desert," he continued, "it'll probably keep chasing us. Before we leave, we'd better settle this."

"And just how are we supposed to settle it?"

"We wait."

And saying that, D went into the depths of the caves. The Hunter was hopelessly indifferent.

Clay and Granny looked at each other.

"I'm gonna take a peek outside," Clay announced. "If I gotta stew in this hole all day, I'll go nuts. If any strange characters start trouble, you'll have to deal with it."

Before Granny could stop him, the man in the blue cap had vanished in the sunlight.

"Dear me, if that man don't have ants in his pants," the old woman griped to herself. "Looks like we're left with just the cool and composed one to rely on now. You really are our guardian angel, you know."

Their guardian angel was deep in the recesses of a hole in the rocks, shrouded in shadows.

"So, what are you folks, anyway?" Lance said meekly. He rubbed his jaw incessantly, which seemed to be something of a habit with him. "I didn't think you were ordinary travelers, but it's like you're all freaks or something. Where are you headed, and what'll you do there?"

"We're pretty much just like you, you know. Relax. We'll get you out of here safe and sound, sure as shooting."

"I sure hope so . . . but I don't even know where the stuff they gave me to eat and drink came from. At this rate, I'll waste away to nothing out here."

"But you were willing to take that chance when you ran away, weren't you? I don't wanna hear such nonsense from a grown man. If you hadn't run into us, you'd have just grit your teeth and forged on, am I right?"

Lance shut his mouth.

"Well, if you're hungry, there's food over in my wagon. Come with me and I'll get you something to eat."

The old woman stood up, and Lance left with her. Only Tae and D remained. D was behind a rock with his eyes closed. About fifteen feet lay between the Hunter and the girl.

"Mrs. Viper just . . ." Tae began to say softly, her face still pointed toward the floor. Her tone was so weak it wouldn't have been at all surprising if it didn't even reach D. "She just left me here. I suppose she thought I'd be safe with you around . . . even though you're the scariest of them all . . ."

There was no reply. Even if Tae's voice was audible, it only would've sounded like incoherent mumbling.

"I never dreamed I'd be able to go home . . . I really thought I'd have to spend the rest of my life in that Noble's castle."

"You remember the Noble's name, don't you?"

When the darkness emitted these words, Tae trembled. It was quite some time before she managed to nod and reply, "Marquis Venessiger . . ."

"Just him?"

"Huh?" Tae cried out softly, turning in D's direction. She could see only darkness.

"Castle Gradinia had a special purpose. Was that the only Noble you met there?"

Tae was silent. Seconds passed. And then, as if unable to bear the silence any longer, she said, "There was another . . . He was taller than the marquis, and more regal . . . I never saw his face, though . . ."

"But his eyes were red. Blazing like rubies."

"Exactly," Tae said, nodding in amazement. But it didn't take long at all for her expression to become completely vacant. She was in the dark. And through that darkness so deep she could even feel the weight of it: two red things were coming closer. A pair of eyes.

"What kind of eyes were they?" D asked, not inquiring at all what sort of man it was.

"Bright red and piercing . . . Eyes that seemed to drink me up, body and soul . . . All they had to do was take one look at me . . .

and then I couldn't even think at all . . . Come to think of it . . ." Tae said in a strangely relaxed tone. "Come to think of it," she repeated, "they were kind of like yours. I wonder why that is? Oh, I know now . . . Because they seemed so terribly sad . . ."

"Did he do anything to you?" D asked, changing his tack unexpectedly.

Tae was horribly shaken. "Not a thing . . . Nothing happened to me . . . I really just met him. Why would you ask me something like that? You're a Hunter, aren't you? Don't ask me anything you don't need to know."

"The one with the red eyes is a ruler." The darkness didn't move in the slightest, but smoldered behind the rocks. "The sun is setting on the Nobility's influence over our world, and yet the gusts from their black wings still bear mystery into so many lives. Yours may be one of them. What did he do?"

"Stop it!" Tae cried, covering her face as she got up. "Nothing happened to me at all. If anything did, I don't remember it—so please don't ask me such horrible questions." Her tone sounded cold enough to freeze a stone.

A tear glittered as it trickled down her cheek. Scattering those sparkling droplets to the wind, Tae raced from the cavern.

A few minutes later, Granny Viper showed up in the cave. "D— you in here?" she called out.

"Over here."

"You said something to the girl, didn't you? She came running back to the wagon, bawling her eyes out, you know," the old woman said in an uninflected tone.

"And that bothers you?"

"A little, I guess. After all, she's valuable merchandise."

"You've been traveling with her a while. Have you noticed any-thing about her?"

"Like what?" Granny asked, a fine thread of tension stitching through her flesh.

"Any physical irregularities? Swings in her mental state?"

"Sure, there's some of that to a degree," Granny replied, her tone already relaxed again. "But then, she's a girl at an impressionable age who's spent quite some time living with the Nobility, and now she's on a long, long journey home. If there wasn't anything weird about her, that in itself would be pretty weird. Look, I'm gonna be on my toes to see to it that nothing strange happens to her until I can hand her over to her family. And I'll thank you to keep any funny remarks to yourself. You should be thinking of some way to get us out of this godforsaken land as soon as possible."

"The girl has to be brought home," said a voice from the darkness. "Her family's still around, I gather."

"Yeah. Her parents passed on not long after she was taken, but her brother and his wife have a farm."

"*Alone* she might've been okay, but the *two of them* are in for a hard life."

"Just what's that supposed to mean?" Granny snapped, a heavy shade of dismay rising in her face.

Hearing a knock, Tae looked up. The forearms her face had been buried in were damp to the elbows. Quickly pawing at the corners of her eyes with the backs of her hands, Tae said, "Come in."

Expecting to see Granny Viper, the girl was actually a bit surprised by who opened her bedroom door. It was Lance. Scratching his head uneasily, he said, "Sorry to bother you. It's just that I heard crying . . ."

"It's nothing."

"Well, if you're okay, then. I was just worried, is all. Well, see you."

"Don't go," Tae cried out reflexively.

Lance didn't know what to say. As he stopped there in spite of himself, his eyes caught Tae crumpling on the bed. "Hey!"

"Don't mind me. Just let me be."

"But you just—" Lance began hesitantly. "I can't just stand idly by when a girl's crying. At times like this you shouldn't be alone. If you had someone to talk to, it'd be—"

"I'm fine, so get out."

Like a razor through the conversation, her tone was so intense Lance finally grasped the situation. "I get it. I'm sorry."

As he slowly turned his back, Tae called out to him huskily, "Wait—" It sounded like her nose was stuffed. "I'm sorry. But I'd just like to be alone. Please."

"Okay. But keep your chin up," Lance said, having nothing but a trite expression for this situation.

"Sure," Tae replied in the brightest tone she could manage.

Donning a smile that suited his bony face, Lance took his leave.

As the door closed, all the strength drained from Tae's body. Her hands rested naturally on her abdomen. A heartrending sigh spilled from her. That sorrowful breath carried the girl's curse on the universe. Her dainty shoulders trembled. Sobbing split her lips. There was little else she could do.

Tae watched as a number of sparkling beads shattered in her lap. Even after those beads had become stains, her eyes didn't move. They had a dangerous hue to them.

Standing, she pulled a leather bag out from under her bed. Her pale hand was swallowed by it, and then came back out with something long and thin and shiny. She tugged on one end with her other hand and it came apart in two pieces—a short knife and a sheath. When her eyes were reflected in the tempered steel, a spark of urgency resided in them.

Slowly the blade rose. At its tip sat Tae's throat. A light push made it dimple the flesh. As the blade moved forward the tiniest bit, its edge was stained red with blood.

Her trembling ceased. A decision had been reached. With the same speed that she raised it, she pulled the knife away again. Tae heaved a heavy sigh.

Just as she finished sheathing the knife, the door flew open without warning. It was Granny Viper. The first thing she saw wasn't Tae's face, but rather what the girl had in her hand. As she wrested the weapon from the girl with incredible force, Granny was probably disappointed by the complete lack of resistance. "Why you—"

"I'm fine. You don't have to worry about me," Tae said in a voice so faint it was barely audible.

An instant later a harsh slap landed on the girl's cheek. Exposed by the way the shock of the blow turned her head, the other cheek resounded with another smack. A wrinkled hand seized the girl by the collar and shook her.

"Listen—and listen good," Granny said, hammering the words into the face of the young girl gazing back at her absentmindedly. "You're valuable merchandise to me. It'd be a hell of a thing if you went off and damaged yourself now. I've got a duty to deliver you to your home without a mark on you. *I'm* responsible for you. And I've always met my responsibilities. Now, I'm not about to let you blemish my tidy reputation, either. You hear me? The next time you pull something like this, I'll forget all about bringing you home and I'll kill you myself. You remember that!"

Tae waited until the old woman had finished her threats. "Please, just kill me," the girl then mumbled.

It took Granny a few seconds to realize what she'd just heard. "What did you say?"

"I never even wanted to go home in the first place. So, if there's anything you don't like about me, go ahead and kill me here and now." Though her tone was hollow, a resolute will lay behind it.

"So, you don't wanna go home then?" Granny said, sounding somewhat obtuse. She wasn't badly flustered. In fact, the look she gave Tae was almost gentle.

Tae was silent. A great weight had suddenly been lifted from her chest.

"Swear to me you won't try any more of this foolishness," Granny bade her in a low voice.

The girl's pale visage was still aimed at the floor. For the longest time, the two of them simply stood there.

Clucking her tongue, the old woman said, "You're an obstinate one. But let me make it perfectly clear I'm pretty obstinate myself about you not doing anything else stupid. I don't care if you try hanging yourself or drinking poison—I'll bring you back to life and deliver you home. I'm not about to let a slip of a girl like you soil the name of Granny Viper. The Nobility did something to you, didn't they?"

Tae's face shot up. "Don't ask me about that," she said.

"Good enough," the old woman said with a nod. "It seems just asking you was effective. Well, I suppose if you've come around that much, you're not likely to do away with yourself so easily. Until we can get across this desert, just keep remembering all the bad things that happened to you."

"As far as memories go—I don't really have any."

"Is that a fact? Then you just have to think about what lies ahead. A person can live without memories if need be."

Tae's eyes shot up to the old woman's face. "Is that what you do, Mrs. Viper?"

"Spare me," Granny Viper said with an exaggerated frown. "I've got hopes and dreams, too, you know. I'm out to make a load of money quick, then open myself a fabric store."

"A fabric store?" Tae said with amazement.

"Yep. It may not look like it now, but I have really fine taste in clothes. See, before I got into this line of work, I had a place in the Capital. I always made children's clothing, and eventually I even made a business out of it."

"A fabric store," Tae muttered once more.

"Traveling together all this time, I've noticed you like kids, don't you?" Granny said in a gentle tone. "And since we're on the subject of fabric, you may as well know there's a sewing machine in the storage compartment under your bed. You can use it if you like."

"Can I really?"

"You can't wear that miserable puss forever. I just said I'd let you borrow my precious sewing machine, and I've never let anyone touch it before. Have to get you to cheer up, anyway. You sure look happy as a pig in slop, but are you sure you know how to use a sewing machine now?"

"When I was back home, I used one a little bit."

"Then give it a shot. But I'm not about to let you use it for free. After all, it wears down on the parts. I was thinking if you had the know-how, I'd have you make me a children's outfit." Indicating the far end of the wagon with her left hand, Granny said, "The material's in there. But if you make a mess of it, your family will have to reimburse me when I turn you over. Okay?"

Not waiting for a response, Granny turned her back. Once she'd reached the door, she looked back.

"I understand the Vampire Hunter might've said some callous things, but don't let it get to you. He might wear a sour puss all the time, but he's not the kind to bully folks. However, he does have to say some hard things to stay true to himself. It's a hard life, being so tough on yourself like that. And I hear it's a lot worse in his case. If you could get inside his skin, it'd be so sad in there it'd kill the likes of you or me."

Tae didn't know what to say.

"Oh, I saw our new arrival coming out of here earlier," the old woman continued. "What was he up to in here?"

"Not a thing. He just came in to cheer me up, is all."

"Hmm, must be nice being a pretty young thing. But I'll have to have a word with him. I can't have you getting all infested with bugs and such."

Granny stepped out of the wagon. A figure in black stood right there.

"Heard us, did you?" the old woman asked.

Not answering, D just put his hand to his traveler's hat and tugged the brim down a bit.

"Here I was, thinking you're cold as ice, and then you go and do something all considerate like coming out from the shade under the wagon for me. You really are worried about the girl, aren't you?"

"Something strange is happening to the desert," D said tersely.

Granny's expression changed. "What?" she asked in equally terse fashion.

"I don't know. Though something's clearly not right, I can't be certain just what it is."

"You saying we should move out, then?"

D didn't answer her, and Granny soon fell silent, too. They'd come to a conclusion about that earlier. For the time being, they could merely wait. D's eyes shifted ever so slightly to the east.

"What is it?" Granny asked, unable to see anything there.

"I hear a sewing machine."

"Looks like she's finally turned around," Granny said with a wry smile. "Now all we have to do is get out of this desert and get away from you."

"From me?"

"I'm sure you're not so thickheaded as to miss what I'm driving at. You're a dangerous man, not just for that girl, but for all women. Hasn't anyone ever told you that? If they haven't, it's because one look at you scrambles their brains."

The old woman stared at D's face, waiting for some reaction. Even out in the sunlight, he looked as beautiful as a crystal that'd formed somewhere in the darkness and then been worked by the chisel of the Almighty. A weird sensation surged up from Granny's lower half, making her shake. The praise of the present world meant nothing to this young man. Only those dead and removed from the material world could pay him his due.

"'There's no place like home,'" D said dispassionately. "At least, that's the maxim of travelers on the Frontier. But is that really the case?"

"I don't necessarily know how relaxing it'll be, but if you've got one, it's generally best you go back to it. You're talking about the girl, aren't you? You trying to suggest I shouldn't bring her home?"

"Are there any hidden who've settled back at home after you delivered them?" the Hunter asked.

"I wouldn't know," Granny said, turning away disdainfully. "I'm only responsible for 'em until I get 'em home. But once they're there, it's somebody else's problem, you see. I'm not really in a position to provide maintenance and upkeep, you know."

"I met one once," D said. His darkness-hued words melted in the sunlight.

Granny gazed vacantly at his beautiful countenance. Unrestrained curiosity and excitement colored her eyes. She couldn't conceive of this young man ever turning his thoughts to the past.

"It was in a village in a southwestern sector of the Frontier. Apparently, he'd been run out of town by the whole community. This boy of about eight was freezing to death by the banks of the river. Not long after I heard the particulars, he died."

"He must've done something or other, right?"

"Don't you see?" said the Hunter.

"No, I don't."

"He didn't do anything at all."

"Is that so? Then, why would they do that?" Granny asked, seeming a bit peeved.

"The boy had been with the Nobility for three months. That was all. A doctor had even verified there was nothing out of the ordinary. He could walk in the daylight, too. And in six months with him, his parents hadn't noticed any strange symptoms."

Granny was at a loss for words.

"However, a certain woman had her suspicions about him, and she went to the mayor and the leader of the Vigilance Committee and complained to them that she'd been bitten. Though they could tell at a glance that the wound had been faked, the two men chose to interpret it differently."

"They wanted to get rid of a nuisance, eh?"

"Within the hour, the whole village was beating down the boy's door. His father was killed trying to stop them, and the house was put to the torch."

"How awful," Granny said, shrugging her shoulders coldly. Tilting her head to one side, she added, "But I'm a bit surprised a lad at death's door could hold out long enough to tell you such an involved tale."

"The explanation came from his mother, who was right by his side."

"So, he had his mum there at the very end to look after him, did he? Well, that's something, isn't it?"

"She was the same woman who'd tipped off the mayor."

White sunlight held the two of them in its embrace. The world was unspeakably peaceful.

Granny awkwardly made her way over to the wagon. "Well, then. We don't have the faintest clue what's bound to happen, but I warrant the safe thing to do is have everything ready for departure. You said there was something strange out there, but do you think it'll be headed this way soon?"

"I don't know," D said, coming out of the shadows.

Granny casually remarked, "I hear it hurts you dhampirs quite a bit to be out in the sunlight. If someone wanted to kill you, daytime would really be the only time to do it. I guess you really can't fight your blood—" the crone said, stopping and clamping one hand over her own mouth mid-sentence.

Her mouth may have been covered, but her feelings showed in her eyes. They were laughing. Laughing maliciously.

Not seeming the least bit bothered, D walked out onto the sea of sand.

"Er, pardon me," Lance said, coming out from behind the rocks to the Hunter's left. Apparently, he'd been keeping out of the sun there ever since Tae had chased him off. D didn't stop walking, so Lance jogged after him. "Your name's D, isn't it?" he asked. "Back in my village, folks used to say that out on the Frontier there was this one incredible Vampire Hunter who was unbelievably handsome. That'd be you, wouldn't it? In which case, the girl and the old woman are connected to your business, right? I mean, I don't know the first thing about this. One of them's unbelievably gloomy, and the other's real testy. Say, speaking of the girl—she wouldn't happen to be one of *the hidden*, would she?"

"What if she is?" D asked as he walked.

"Hey, it doesn't matter to me. But shouldn't you be comforting her or something? She's had it bad enough up till now, and no matter where she goes, folks will give her a hard time if they find out what happened to her. The least you could do is be nice to her until she gets where she's going."

D stopped in his tracks and looked at Lance. "And why are you telling me this?" he asked.

Lance diverted his gaze. His cheeks wore a thin flush—even men blushed when they were subjected to D's gaze. Coughing, he replied, "Well, because you're the only one for the job. Girls her age always fall for the good-looking guys. I guarantee you that. And given that, you're far and away the top out of the three men here. Why don't you spend some time with her? I saw her crying earlier. A girl like her doesn't deserve to suffer like that."

D watched the man without saying a word. Soon he turned to face the desert. It was an endless sea of sand. "Don't leave this spot," he told Lance in a low voice.

Leaving the other man behind as he nodded his agreement, the Hunter advanced about twenty paces, and then stopped. As his face slowly scanned to his right and to his left, there wasn't a trace of tension on it.

"Well, there's something wrong here, and then again there isn't," said a hoarse voice that slipped from the vicinity of his left hand. "But something's sure to happen all right. Better be damn careful."

At that instant, darkness hid the sky. D's coat had fluttered out around him. As he whipped around, his eyes found nothing. There was naught but waves of sand dunes slumbering out in the white sunlight. Lance wasn't there, nor was the old woman and her wagon. Even the rocky mound was gone.

"Oh, boy," D's left hand moaned. "Just perfect. We've been hit with another psi attack."

Psi Attack

CHAPTER 4

I

H ow strong is the attack?" D asked, not sounding at all distressed.

"As if you couldn't tell already. Well, I'd say it's about five thousand rigels on the Noble scale. Enough to drive the entire population of a city mad in a millisecond."

"The desert doesn't pull any punches."

"You said it," the laughter-tinged voice concurred. Both he and the Hunter had far more nerve than any human.

The sound of the wind died out.

D looked down at his feet; waves were lapping at them. His entire field of view was filled by an expanse of deep blue sea. Crests broke here and there, turning the rays of the sun into droplets of light. It looked as though the trip across it would span thousands of miles.

"And the purpose of all this—well, I guess it's to gauge your abilities. What are you gonna do?"

Giving no reply to the voice's query, D stood there. His legs then went into motion. The waves pulled away. Before the sea could help it, the Hunter was waist-deep in the water. The waves were sensors, and their very movements most likely served to relay the results of this test.

"Very interesting," the voice chortled. "So, the desert is a sea, then? Seems it's trying to surprise you, but we'll see who gets a surprise."

Even before the voice had finished speaking, the veracity of its claim became evident. A "feeling" that certainly seemed like astonishment raced across the surface of the sea around D. Silence shrouded the world.

"Looks like it doesn't know quite what to make of you," the voice said, seemingly beside itself with joy. "It's times like these it pays to stick around with you. So, what move will it make?"

D supplied the answer. He was gazing at one spot in the sea. A white wake was drawing closer at a considerable speed.

"Here it comes. There's a shark in the water."

Whether or not D knew what the voice was pointing out, he remained stock-still.

The range was about fifty yards. Forty yards . . . Thirty . . . Twenty . . .

The wake faded into nothingness. Whatever had been knifing through the surface must've gone back underwater.

"Gotta stay on your toes. Your opponent's only an illusion," the voice told D. "You'll have to beat it with just your psyche. Carving it up won't do you any good."

Suddenly, the surface of the water bubbled up. The dark blue form of a fish broke the surface as it leapt into the air. It was a streamlined behemoth, nearly twelve feet long and weighing a good five hundred pounds. The front end had a gigantic mouth open wide and a red gullet. The teeth were like white spearheads.

A flash of silver tore through the entire body. D ducked ever so slightly, and the colossal fish split in two over his head, dropping into the water with an incredible plume of spray. Watery beads reflecting the white sunlight quickly turned to purple with the fresh blood spilling from the beast.

However, D's eyes were drawn to the two bloody trails running behind the creature. The trails had drawn closer together almost instantly, converging to form a single wake that began leisurely circling D.

"Looks like the other side's no slouch, either," the voice said, its tone tense. "If your mental powers beat it, we should've gone back where we were the second you sliced into that thing. But since it didn't play out that way, this could be trouble. You can kill this thing over and over, and it'll just keep coming."

D's reply was placid. "Still, it has to die eventually. Even if it's just an illusion."

"Kill a dream?" the voice snickered. "I suppose *you* probably could, at that. Here it comes!"

The wake died out; D felt the wall of water pushing against his lower body. Apparently his foe intended to attack from underwater. Deadly as D's blade might be, its speed and power would be halved when underwater. In that respect, the phantasmal sea would be real enough.

D sank below the surface. Shifting his sword to his left hip, the Hunter was poised like those who drew and struck from the waist. The movements of the water relayed the speed and distance of his foe—and for a second, a flash of crimson zipped right by D. In stark contrast to the blue sky, the streak didn't fade for the longest time. The Hunter's submerged foe writhed in agony.

A second later, the world went black.

His long, gorgeous shadow stretched across the white sands.

"Wow," the voice said in a hushed tone. "Good work. But who in the world did that . . . ?"

D turned to face the person he sensed coming up behind him.

"You okay?" Granny asked, still breathing heavily as she held the blunderbuss ready. "You were acting kind of funny, and the sand sort of welled up out there and was making a beeline for you, so I put a round into it. What the hell was that thing anyway?"

"A shark."

"Huh?" the old woman said, her eyes wide in disbelief.

D turned back to the rocky mound as if nothing had happened at all.

Lance was still standing where the Hunter had left him. "What in the world—" he muttered like a mental defective, wiping the sweat from his brow. "You were standing there stock-still the whole time, so I figured you were up to something, and then all of a sudden you pulled out your sword and *Whap!* Of course, I couldn't exactly catch you drawing your blade, though. What on earth did you lay into?"

"A shark."

"What?!" Lance exclaimed, mouth dropping open.

"You mean to say you didn't see it?"

"Nope."

D turned his back to the man.

"What'll we do next?" Granny asked apprehensively.

"We wait." And with that alone as his reply, D returned to the cave.

Evening came. But something was missing: Clay. He'd gone out, but had never returned.

"What do you suppose happened to him?" Granny said with seeming concern, but she was actually more worried about losing some of their muscle than about Clay's safety as such. D didn't seem to care much at all. "You think maybe the desert finished him off? Well? Do you?" the old woman asked. "I don't believe this! If you're not the coldest customer ever. We're all in this together now. The least you could do is show a little concern, you know."

"You took it upon yourselves to follow me," D said. He'd merged with the darkness in the depths of the cave. The lamp Granny had in her hand was the only source of light, and it threw an orange veil over her surroundings.

"True enough," the crone replied, "but you could come up with a little nicer way of putting it, I'm sure. If push comes to shove, you plan on taking off and leaving us behind?"

"It's up to you whether you come or not. I'll let you know when I'm leaving. That's it."

"Curse you," Granny shouted, stomping her feet in anger. "I'm not out here alone, you know. You mean to tell me you're not worried about Tae?"

"How is she?"

"See! I just knew you were!" Granny exclaimed, breaking into a grin at her own cleverness. "I don't care how cold you might look; you've got redder human blood running in your veins than any of us. And it's warm, too. My guess is it's a lot warmer than most folks'. Relax. The girl's been fixed on mastering that sewing machine since noontime. She learned how to use one before, and she's sure got a knack for it. I warrant she'll have an outfit finished pretty soon."

"What's she making?" D inquired.

"Actually—" Granny said, hemming and hawing a bit, "—she's not about to show anyone."

"If our foe is coming for us, it'll be tonight. If nothing's happened by dawn, we'll move out. You're all set, aren't you?"

"Good to go anytime!"

As Granny replied, someone moved around outside the cave.

"Hey there!" a voice called out.

Jumping nearly three feet in the air, Granny brought her hand to the jar on her hip. As for D, he must've sensed the new arrival, because he didn't move an inch. It was Clay.

"Sure took your sweet time coming back, didn't you?" Granny said sharply, with a trenchant look that matched her voice. She may have already noticed that something wasn't right.

"There's something I want to show you all. Come with me," Clay said in a tone that was as stiff as a board. It was clear at a glance he was under some sort of spell.

"It's come, sure enough. It's come to get us," the old woman groaned. "What'll we do, D?"

The darkness to the rear took on human form, and Clay turned around and slowly headed back the way he'd come. D followed after him. He didn't even glance at Granny.

Outside was a land of darkness.

"Just a second. What about the other two?" the old woman asked Clay.

"They've already been taken away."

Granny's eyes bulged in their sockets. The fact that their foe could abduct the two of them without her noticing, let alone D, was simply mind-boggling. Teeth grinding together fiercely, she reached for her jar with her right hand.

"Later," D told her.

"Why wait?! If we grab him now, it'll be easy enough to get him to spill where the other two are. It goes against my grain to just waltz into whatever the enemy's got set up for me."

"He's not what we're up against; whoever's controlling him is. Break the spell over him now, and we'll be left with a man who doesn't know anything."

Granny let the strength drain from her form. The Hunter's assessment of the situation was sound. Her hand came away from the jar.

The three set off into the desert; there was nothing but sand. The moon was out. With every step they took, the ground made a strangely plaintive sound. Clay continued on without hesitation—surely whoever controlled him was also taking care of his sense of direction.

The rocky mound had long since been swallowed by darkness. They'd walked for perhaps thirty minutes and then Clay halted.

They were out in the middle of the desert—nothing but the shadows of the three of them stretched across the silvery sands. Suddenly, there was a voice in D and Granny's heads. Neither the sex nor age of the speaker was clear. They couldn't even tell whether or not it was an organic being.

I have never encountered beings—humans—like you before. It would appear there are all manner of things beyond my world.

"What have you done with the others?" Granny shouted as she looked all around. "One of 'em I could care less about, but the girl's valuable property of mine. If you've done anything to her, it won't end well for you."

I'm currently inspecting the one to which you refer. Quite an interesting human specimen.

"Hmph! If you're so interested in humans, you had all the time in the world to study Lance. Oh, I get it. First time you've ever seen a girl, right?"

No.

"Well, it doesn't matter either way. Where's the girl now? You're gonna give her right back to me. And then you're gonna let us go on our way without any more trouble. After you tell us how to get where we're headed, of course."

The voice fell silent. Back out of the darkness came a feeling that someone was mocking them. But that ended in a heartbeat. A voice deeper than the darkness made sure of that.

"Are you the desert itself?" D asked, still gazing straight ahead. Unlike Granny, he wasn't wound tight. However, the one he addressed knew that if the need arose, every inch of the Hunter would be transformed into a spring of coiled steel.

Yes, the voice replied a bit tardily.

"How long have you been sentient?"

I don't know. But if someone could tell me, I would very much like to know.

"What do you plan on doing with us? Get information from us, or keep us like pets for the rest of our lives like you did with the man?"

I wouldn't do that to you. Or rather, I couldn't. Even if I tried to, you wouldn't let me. You're so dangerous, the other humans can't begin to compare to you.

"Then what will you do?"

I put the very same question to you.

"Leave."

Once again, both sides were enveloped by silence. The sandy plain had nothing to say, but listened intently.

Very well, the voice said without emotion. *I'm aware it would be extremely dangerous to fight you. I will do nothing, and neither will you.*

"I'm going to leave now."

Do as you like. I'll seek the information I desire from the rest of them.

"Hold on there just a minute," Granny said, throwing a stern gaze at the young man in black. "Don't tell me you plan on pulling out and leaving all of us here."

"I don't have any plans one way or the other. The rest of you just followed after me."

"Okay. Then we'll follow along after you now, too. You wouldn't have a problem with that, would you? And if we run into trouble, help us out."

Suddenly Granny's body grew rigid.

I still have business with the rest of you.

The crone's head rung with same voice D heard.

I'll dispose of the man for his treachery, but I should like to investigate you and the other two at greater length. Come to me.

"Help me, D!" the old woman shrieked. The sand was up around her ankles. She was sinking. "D!" Granny cried.

Go in peace, the voice told D. *I would do nothing that might snuff their lives. These are the precious samples that will allow me to learn about human beings.*

Let me ask you something, D said without using his voice. *What will you do once you've learned about humans?*

Say no more, and be gone. You should consider yourself fortunate to be allowed to leave in one piece.

One more thing—what were those globes and butterflies for?

They were tools to ascertain your whereabouts. When the globes proved ineffective, I sent the butterflies. On seeing those patterns, the brain gives off special radio waves.

"Help, D!" Granny shrieked from down by his feet. "Forget about me, but save the girl—save Tae!"

A gag spilled from her throat, and the old woman's head sank into the sand. Clay disappeared right after her. A funnel-shaped depression remained for a moment, but sand soon tumbled in from all sides to fill it again.

Not even reaching out for them with his hand, D simply stared at the sandy surface, but then quickly started to walk back to the rocky mound. After a few steps, he halted. Slowly turning, he headed back the way he'd just come.

You are a fool, the voice scoffed, the hostility naked in its tone. *Reconsider what you're doing. A battle between us is in neither of our best interests.*

Naturally, there was no reply.

Standing in the spot where Granny had disappeared, D raised his left hand.

An intense turbulence spread from somewhere unseen.

Stop it, the voice said.

At the very same time, both heaven and earth howled. The snarling winds turned hard as steel and slammed against D, carrying him away. Caught in a massive gust, he flew far across the desert. The wind was blowing at speeds of well over a hundred miles an hour.

D's left hand hadn't come down. Fingers spread wide, his palm was suddenly filled by someone's face: a face with sarcastic eyes, an aquiline nose, and a tiny mouth. As soon as that mouth opened, it instantly swallowed the howling winds.

His foe had lost the strength to speak, while D stood there without making a sound.

"Good stuff," a hoarse voice said. "This wind is pretty damn tasty!"

Sailing back down to earth as swiftly as the gale had carried him off, D turned his left hand to the ground, toward the spot that had swallowed the old woman. If Granny Viper had been there to see the tiny lips pucker, even she would've been shocked—even more so when a powerful new gale rushed from those same lips.

The sand shot away. In no time at all, a hole six feet in diameter had been dug in the ground.

Stop it! the voice exclaimed, the words exploding in D's head. *Stop it! Stop it! Stop it!*

A heartbeat later, the figure in black was swallowed by the earth.

II

For several seconds, he was aware of traveling down through the sand. Just as the sand's resistance ended, D's speed increased, and the Hunter landed on his feet on a firm base. It was a stone floor. Incredible mass surrounded him on all sides. He was in a large subterranean cavern—a natural one.

So, you've come, have you? Fool.

Oblivious to the condescending remark, D surveyed his surroundings dispassionately, and then soon angled off into the darkness to his right. Was it that absurdly easy for the young man to tell where his abducted compatriots were? He was surrounded by true darkness, yet he walked impassively through it. The blackness was so thick that it seemed not even light itself could ever penetrate it. It took about fifty seconds for his eyes to find human forms there: four figures lay on the stone floor. As he walked toward them, the air before him stirred.

Something buzzed through the air. Giving a scream, it fell at D's feet in its death throes. At first glance, the winged creature was built like an evil sprite. Though it no doubt made flight easier, its body was disturbingly thin. The fangs jutting from its mouth—and the claws stretching from its fingertips—hadn't escaped D's notice, either.

One thing after another ripped through the air. If there'd been the slightest bit of light, the deadly little oddities zipping at D from all directions would've been apparent, as would D's consummate fighting skill. There was no telling when he'd drawn his longsword, but the elegant blade danced in his hand, sending each and every one of his attackers crashing to the ground.

Not bothering to sheathe his sword, D walked forward. Suddenly, there was nothing there for his foot to rest on. The ground had opened wide. In a fraction of a second, D kicked off the ground with his other leg. As he was leaping, he lost his balance, and the earth continued to crack open. D began to descend instead. Unable to correct his form, he couldn't get much distance from his leap. Into the abyss his body dropped.

The Hunter's left hand reached out, only narrowly catching hold of the lip of the ever-widening gap. D sprang up at once. Just as his two feet touched back down on the floor, the crevice stopped growing. D turned around. His darkness-piercing eyes found the ground still lay there, innocent in every regard. It'd all been a psychological attack. If he'd fallen into that nonexistent pit, his own belief in it might've kept him falling for all eternity.

D went over to the other four and knelt by Tae's side. His left hand hovered over her lips—her breathing was normal. The same hand moved to her brow. He must've employed a trick of some sort, because Tae's eyes then opened.

"You okay?" D asked succinctly.

Tae latched onto his arm with both hands. "D—is that you?" she asked.

"Yes."

"I can't see anything at all. Where are we?"

"Underground," the Hunter replied. "Can you walk?"

"Yeah."

Still clinging to D's arm, Tae got to her feet as fast as the Hunter rose again.

"Wait here," D told her. "I'll go wake the others."

"No. I don't want you to leave me alone in the pitch black," Tae said, refusing to relinquish her hold on him.

"Okay, grab onto my coat then," the Hunter told her. Still, the girl wouldn't move. Reaching up with his right hand to where Tae clung to him near the shoulder, D caught hold of her wrists. Speechless, the girl trembled slightly. Once both her hands had been pushed down by D's waist, Tae took a tight grip of his coat.

Whether or not D noticed how flushed her face was in the darkness was anyone's guess.

The Hunter's left hand pressed against the foreheads of the other three, waking each of them in turn. Unlike Tae, all three of them immediately grasped their situation.

It was Granny who asked, "Is there a way out of here?"

"I don't know," D replied with his habitual bluntness. "We're underground, but it could be we're not really."

"What?!" Clay said, eyes bulging, although no one but D could actually tell that. "What's that supposed to mean? Oh, I see—this is some kind of mind game, eh? Very fucking impressive."

"Real or not, how are we supposed to get back to the surface?" Granny asked.

"That's obvious," said Clay. "We settle the hash of whoever's running all this. Hey, Lance . . . you there?"

"Yeah."

"You sure you don't have some idea where we can find him?"

"Not a clue."

"Sheesh, you're worthless," Clay spat. "Well, never mind. He's gotta be hiding around here somewhere, and I'll ferret him out soon enough. Hey, Hunter—move everyone back behind me. I'm gonna pluck me a tune."

Harp in hand, Clay stood up.

"I'll be using my focused sonic waves of destruction. Might make you a little nauseous, gang, but just suck it up."

His coarse fingers touched the fearsome musical instrument.

It was at that moment that light sprang up in the darkness. All around the other four, countless globes of light had winked on. At long last the four of them could see each other's faces.

"Not those . . ." Lance groaned.

"Recognize these things, do you?" Granny asked.

"Yeah. Those are the same things that showed up the night they first brought me back. They're guards. One touch and you're paralyzed."

"Really? Then they gotta be like the hands and feet of whoever controls them," Clay said, licking his chops.

Seeming to sense something in the warrior's tone, Tae clung tightly to the Hunter's black coat.

"This'll be fun. I'm gonna give this thing a good long lesson in what you get for trying to use good ol' humans as guinea pigs. Have some of this!"

A note of unearthly beauty shot off, with death as its passenger. The globes of light directly in front of Clay shattered without a sound.

"Serves you right," the warrior sneered when he sensed obvious pain from nowhere in particular.

"Get 'im!" Granny shouted encouragingly.

"You got it!" Clay replied, spinning around. But a scream from Tae froze him solid.

"Why, what is it?" Granny asked, seeming terribly upset as she turned around. A second later, the old woman's eyes opened wide.

The same cry of "Monster!" flew from both Granny and Lance's mouths.

Still clinging to D, Tae screamed again when she looked up at him.

"Close your eyes!" said a steely voice that knifed through the maddening darkness. Low though it was, it had the power to make all of them comply. "It's just a psi attack that makes each of us look like a monster to the others. Don't open your eyes again until I tell you to."

Eyes shut tight, Clay turned in D's direction. A shout split his lips, a battle cry of "Goddamn freak!" In unison with his cry his right hand danced, wringing the sweet sounds of death from the instrument at his waist.

Zipping over Tae's head after D shoved her out of the way, the ultrasonic waves disappeared into the darkness. Somewhere out there, something collapsed.

"D, I still see it, even with my eyes shut!" Granny Viper shouted, her face pale.

"Look down," D told them, and then he leapt.

Darkness melted into darkness. Only D's perfect pale countenance revealed his location. Sailing over Clay's head as he made ready to recklessly launch another note from his harp, the Hunter landed right behind the warrior. Screaming, Clay spun around. He wore a crazed look. D's sword limned an arc as it came off his back.

In both narrowly evading the blade and leaping a good distance away, the younger Bullow truly deserved to be counted among the most renowned warriors of the Frontier. However, just as Clay came back to earth, a dull thud echoed from the back of his head. Before the warrior could launch any more ultrasonic waves at whatever he thought his pitch-black retinas reflected, he unceremoniously collapsed to the floor.

"Got 'im!" Granny was heard to exclaim.

D's eyes discerned the old woman standing there, still facing down but with an old-fashioned firearm in one hand. Tae and Lance were lying on the ground—that was the best possible solution.

"Is this a psi attack?" Granny asked.

"That's right."

"What should we do?"

"Stop it," D replied tersely.

"Good," Granny replied, sounding like she must've had the biggest grin imaginable plastered on her face. She was eager to counter-attack. "What do you suppose it'll throw at us next?" As she spoke, she unconsciously looked around her. "Hey, everything seems normal now . . . which basically means I can't see anything at all again," she said.

In response, D told her, "Here comes the next one."

"What?!" As Granny frantically spun around again, two figures emerging from the depths of the darkness entered her field of view. Dimmer than the very blackness, one was faintly recognizable even in this murk. The one on the right wore a wide-brimmed hat, and the hem of his coat fluttered in a dark breeze. Spying the much smaller figure with wild, disheveled hair, Granny muttered, "It's me—and D."

Perhaps D had already realized the truth. He took the sword he had in hand and put it back in its sheath. It clinked home with a beautiful sound.

"Are they illusions?" Granny asked, poised for battle.

That's very perceptive of you, the voice said. *But they are no mere phantasms. As you shall see.*

Was the purr of a blade through the air faster? Or was Granny swifter as she leapt out of the way? Still poised for action as if nothing had happened, the old woman now had two blackish streaks dripping down her deeply wrinkled face. Real blood.

That blood should be flowing through your veins. Even in a world of dreams, death may come. Here, reality itself is little more than a dream. If you believe you've been cut and think you'll bleed, then bleed you truly shall, just as you see. The two of them were created using all the data I currently have on you, but I believe you'll find their strength and constitution are perfectly matched against your own in virtually every regard. Meaning neither you nor they could ever win or lose to the other in all eternity. I look forward to seeing what sort of fight it will be.

The false D leapt. Coming from above with his full body weight and all his speed added to that of his blade, he brought a blow down at the top of D's head. The painful sound of metal-on-metal gave way to blue sparks that shot through the air.

Keeping his freshly drawn blade at the same height as when it'd parried his foe's deadly attack, D made a horizontal slash with the longsword. It met with nothing. His foe was D, too.

The two figures glared at each other across a gap of less than ten feet. Who would make the next move?

Knowing all the tricks his foe possessed, the false D readied his sword nonetheless. Seeing that a prolonged battle would be to his disadvantage, he intended to gamble everything on one lethal blow. The air whistled with a slash from above one shoulder to just below the other. He was close enough for that attack to actually work.

D took a step forward. As he did so, he simultaneously brought out his sword. The instant the false D's blow had bitten into his shoulder, the tip of D's blade could be seen slipping into his opponent's chest.

"Not bad," D said. Just as he'd taken a step forward to throw off the balance of the false D's attack, so his foe had managed to avoid a thrust through the heart by the merest fraction of an inch—an exquisite move executed in a hundredth of a second. Apparently, what the voice had told him was no lie. The two of them were deadlocked. Whoever made the next move would die.

They leapt in unison. Streaks of light crossed in midair. The sound of blades knifing through the wind only followed later.

As D landed, a black line split his forehead—the work of a blow from his foe's blade as they flew past each other. His foe smirked at him. No one save D could see the torrent of fresh blood spilling down his opponent's clothes from the horizontal slash across the false D's chest. Such was the difference between fighting with a shoulder wound versus a hole in the chest.

His opponent dashed into action.

D's field of view wavered—one of the streams of blood running from his forehead had changed direction and run into his right eye. The blade meant to meet his foe was off ever so slightly, shaving the flesh from his opponent's cheek while the flashing steel of the false D pierced the real D's heart. As D dropped to his knees without uttering a word, the callous blade was driven in much, much deeper from above.

That finishes him, then, the voice said wearily.

But who would've thought the voice would gasp just then, or that the false D's eyes would go wide with astonishment? His foe watched as a hand gloved in black grabbed his blade from below.

D raised his face. His eyes gave off a reddish light.

You couldn't be . . .

Strength surged into D's lower body. Perhaps the Noble blood that coursed through the young man's veins gave him unnatural power, for even after being pierced through the heart, he was very slowly rising to his feet.

His opponent struggled to pull the blade free or force it in deeper. It didn't move an inch. The balance of power had been broken.

A low moan spilled from D's lips. Something else accompanied it—a pair of fangs. Did his foe see how the tracks of the rolling drops of blood from his forehead vanished at his lips?

When his opponent tried to leap away, it was a second too late, and D's blade came straight down to split the other man's head. Whipping around in a flash, the same sword then pierced his opponent's heart. His foe crumbled to the ground.

Expressionless though he was, D somehow seemed satisfied with the way the false D's countenance had never betrayed any terror even at the bitter end, when his head turned to dust.

The pressure of the darkness was suddenly gone. D was gazing down at his feet and the shadow he cast there. It fell across silver sand.

Having slain the phantasm his foe had conjured, he'd thwarted the psychological attack. There was no sword through his chest, no blood coursing from his brow, but he was still holding his longsword. The psi attack had been ingenious; it had managed to rouse D's demonic nature. But had even *that* part been real?

"That was a hell of a scary character to deal with. I mean, whoever made him, of course," a low, decrepit voice commented from somewhere around D. "With all the power it invested in that, I'd wager it took a terrible hit just now. If you plan on getting out of here, now would be the perfect time for it."

Not replying, D looked around at their surroundings. Three figures were stretched out on the sand. A diminutive fourth stood ready for battle: Granny Viper. She was probably still squaring off against an opponent. Apparently, the psychological assault had affected her much more than it had D.

D returned his longsword to the sheath on his back. At the pleasant metallic song of it sliding into its sheath, Granny shuddered a bit. Dazedly, she surveyed her surroundings. Noticing D first, she blinked her eyes. "What on earth did you—? Why, I was fighting right here and . . . Oh, I get it—you broke the psi attack, didn't you?"

She quickly turned and looked for Tae, a show of her sincere devotion to the job. Racing over to the girl with a cry that bordered on a scream, the very first thing she did was check for a pulse. Having enough foresight to take the possibility of internal injuries into consideration, she was careful not to move the girl too much.

Seeing the crone's shoulders come down in manifest relief, D then turned his eyes to the heavens. The moon was visible in the clear sky. D began walking back toward the rocky mound. "You can handle the rest," he told Granny. "We leave in twenty minutes."

III

Three hours later, the horizon donned a tinge of blue. In lieu of a rising sun, the air filled with rising winds. The hard-flung grains of sand beat against the wagon's canopy mercilessly, making a sound like the peal of a bell. Granny spat a grit-laden wad of saliva from the driver's seat. Both D and Clay had scarves to shield their nose and mouth, and they rode on either side of the wagon. The vehicle was renowned for its ability to reach speeds of seventy-five miles per hour on level ground, but now it barely managed a tenth of that.

Granny was anxious—the damage D had dealt their enemy wouldn't be enough to destroy it. Once its wounds had healed, it was sure to make its next move against them. If it threw out another tornado, they'd be right back where they started from; in fact, some result even more miserable definitely lay ahead for them. You could say the first order of business was to get as far away as they could before their foe had a chance to recover. In her heart of hearts, the crone prayed the enemy's power didn't extend across the entire desert.

But the real question was, just where were they racing now? Though they knew the direction they were headed, their present location was a mystery.

D was riding ahead of the wagon and off to the right, and as Granny gazed at his back, she had a strange look in her eye. According to the Vampire Hunter, the town they were bound for lay more than a hundred miles south by southwest of there. She'd asked him just how he knew for sure, but he hadn't answered her. Ordinarily, she'd have accused him of pulling her leg and raised a big stink. Even Granny herself wasn't sure yet why she'd let the matter rest so easily. She knew he was a dhampir. There was no need to be surprised when a man with the blood of the Nobility in his veins displayed such an incredible ability. However, she got the impression there was more to this young man than this fact alone.

Granny was quite familiar with ordinary dhampirs. While it was true that they were several ranks above humans, they still had their limits. If you tried hard enough and were willing to die in the process, you could even kill one. But that reasoning didn't seem to apply in the least to the gorgeous young man before her. Could he be killed? The very thought of it had never occurred to her. Like darkness given form, the young man could send any opponent at all into the depths of the abyss, if he so wished. From her own intuition, Granny realized the Hunter's knowledge was surely instinctive as well.

Finding something disturbing about the black back of the man they were supposed to be relying on, Granny finally decided to speak to him. "Tell me something, D. Just what do we have to do to stop this desert once and for all?"

As she expected, she got no reply. But she did hear another voice from off to her left.

"Sheesh, how the hell would he know? How could anybody possibly know anything that crazy?" Perhaps feeling somewhat humiliated after learning from the old woman that he'd been used like a puppet on a string, Clay sounded more vindictive than ever.

Granny just smiled sweetly at him and cooed, "Now, don't go saying that. After all, he had a little part in saving you, you know."

"Hmph. I'll square things up with him sooner or later." Clay then turned and looked at the wagon. "All that aside, you sure it's a good idea having them two riding in there together? That sodbuster might look all well-behaved, but down deep he could just be some hot-handed operator for all we know."

"We don't really have a choice. Unlike you, the two of them are ordinary folks. See, they still haven't shaken off all the aftereffects of the psi attack. But just let me warn you—"

"I know already! If I go touching your precious goods, you ain't responsible for what happens next, right? Shit, if you're that worried about it, why don't you put a chain around her neck and keep a hold on one end of it? I ain't promising you a damn thing. To tell the truth, I've always wondered what it'd be like to put it to one of *the hidden*. Oops..." Clay said, smirking as he pulled away. No doubt he'd felt the urge to kill radiating from every inch of the old woman.

Turning forward again with a disapproving cluck of her tongue, Granny then stiffened with tension. D had come to a halt. "What's wrong?" the old woman asked with fear in her voice, though that was just a part of a plot she'd set in motion to get his pity.

"It's a sandstorm. A little more than a mile ahead of us."

"Not a twister?"

"No, a sandstorm."

The old woman squinted her eyes. "Well, I can't see anything."

"If we keep going straight, we'll run right into it," said D. "This calls for a detour."

"But, wouldn't that put us behind schedule? I mean, that'd be a problem for you too, right?"

"If we're lucky, it's just a normal sandstorm."

"Stop feeding us this load of crap," Clay snapped. "I don't see a damn thing either."

"I can see it."

That one softly spoken phrase was enough to silence even the irrepressible Clay.

"Or would you rather try and risk it?" the Hunter ventured.

"Great idea!" the old woman exclaimed, slapping her knee noisily. "That's just what we'll have to do. I mean, what's a sandstorm or two? Let a little thing like that stop you, and you could hardly call yourself a man the rest of your days."

"You gotta be shitting me. I'm completely against this," Clay groused.

"Oh my! I thought you were one of the greatest warriors on the Frontier, but I guess you ain't all you're cracked up to be."

Granny's retort brought immediate results. Blood rushed into Clay's face. "Don't make me laugh," he snarled. "I ain't saying I'm afraid. I just gotta find my brother, is all."

"Oh, you poor thing, you. Say, D—how far is it from here to the place we got scooped up?"

"About seventy miles, I'd say."

"Now, I don't care how chock full of fraternal love you are when you gallop off, you won't be able to cover that kind of distance. You'll just have to leave your brother's fate to the heavens. If luck is on your side, who knows—you could run into him again somewhere outside the desert in two or three years. And if it's against you, he'll bake in the sun and die like a dog."

At that point, a bizarre reaction came over Clay. A smile that really had no business on a wild beast of a man like him—a smile some might even call spooky—spread across his whole face. "My brother Bingo baking in the sun? Did you say something about dying? That's just too funny. I'd sure as hell like to see that with my own two eyes," he spoke in a voice like a corpse, with a grin that was almost unimaginable from someone with such a ruthless, fearless image. Even Granny's expression grew stiff.

Just then, the back door of the wagon suddenly started to open, leaving the crone at a loss for words.

Scrambling down the built-in set of steps, the pale figure kicked up the sand as she ran down the right side of the wagon.

"Tae!" Granny shouted, standing like a vengeful demon. "Get her for me, D!"

In response to her cry, the Hunter wheeled his cyborg horse around. It was a heartbeat later that the horse tumbled forward, just as he was about to gallop off. From its back a figure in black flew like a mystic bird. Landing in a spot some fifteen feet away, D plunged the sword he'd already drawn deep into sand at his feet.

"What's going on?" Clay asked as he looked all around.

"It looks like it's come back around," D told the younger Bullow. While he was speaking, the figure of Tae dwindled between the dunes with a speed never anticipated from such dainty little legs.

"Wait up, Miss Tae!" Lance cried, clutching his head as he tumbled from the back of the wagon.

"What on earth happened?"

Stopped short by the question Granny had barked, he replied in an almost tearful tone, "I don't know. We were talking, and then all of a sudden she whacked me over the head with a wrench."

"You stay right there. I'll do something about this," the old woman said. Still standing in the same spot, she reached for her jar with her right hand. D, however, didn't move, and Tae just kept getting farther away—she was already more than a hundred yards from the wagon.

Granny's hand came out of the jar balled in a fist. From behind her, Clay saw that countless multicolored particles had begun to trickle smoothly from between her clenched fingers, but the flow quickly ended. And just what had become of those particles that fell on the floor of the front seat by Granny's feet and down onto the desert sands? Driven by what might be called a warrior's instinctive curiosity, the younger Bullow was just about to spur his mount forward when Granny bent low. For a split second, it seemed like a flash of blue light shot by her feet.

Tae was just about to disappear behind a dune. Seeing the way the girl collapsed completely made Lance's eyes bulge out of their sockets.

"D—how're things over there?" Granny cried out.

"Better for the moment."

Apparently it was no exaggeration, as the Hunter's cyborg horse had gotten back up and was shaking off the grains of sand.

"In that case, go! The girl's out cold."

The figure in black dashed off, coat fanning around him.

"What did you do, old lady? What the hell is that sand, anyway?"

Granny turned and smiled at Clay's query. "That's a trade secret," she replied.

"Don't give me any of that crap!"

"It is, just as sure as your little tricks are."

By that, she clearly meant the way he did battle. The gazes of the two—ferocious and cruel—collided in midair in a shower of unseen sparks.

D scooped up Tae. The reason she'd collapsed so suddenly surely had something to do with the crone's mysterious skill, although D didn't know exactly what that was. Judging from the way Tae's hair stood on end, she must've been hit with some sort of electric shock. However, D had seen with his own eyes that nothing had passed between the old woman and the girl. How, then, had it happened?

A light tap on her cheek, and Tae quickly opened her eyes. "D?" she said.

"Don't move. What happened?"

"I don't know," Tae replied, her eyes tinged with terror. "I was talking with Mr. Lance, when I just got this feeling that I had to get out of there. This voice was telling me to go outside—"

It was clear then that the desert had indeed returned to the way it had been.

D reached out with one hand to pull the girl up, and behind him a flume of sand shot up unexpectedly. Not simply sand, this had a humanoid shape. Tae's eyes were wide open now, and they caught the silvery flash of light that shot through the air. The outline of the figure that'd pushed just its upper body from the ground suddenly crumbled, and a heartbeat later it was again a golden pile of sand melting back into the desert. Tae gave a scream.

To either side of them the sand rose in one place after another, taking human form everywhere it did. The forms almost looked like the miasma rising from a solidified swamp. Pole-thin arms reached for D's neck.

The silver flash that shot up diagonally took the limbs off at the elbow. When all of their arms had fallen to ground, the shapes flopped backward in what seemed like pain and slowly sank back into the earth.

"There're still more of them," Tae said, her eyes reflecting the countless round heads springing from the sea of sand around them. Would they be able to get back to the wagon? A hundred yards seemed completely hopeless.

A powerful arm wrapped around the girl's waist. As Tae gazed at the gorgeous visage of her sturdy guardian, his name came to her lips. Her anxiety burned away like a fog.

"Here we go," said the Vampire Hunter.

"Okay," Tae replied. She was no longer afraid.

A cloud of dusty creatures was closing in on them. Their heads lacked eyes or noses or mouths. Their bodies were like short, fat rocks with a couple of logs stuck in them, but completely smooth. These unsettling interpretations of the human form were more than six feet tall and born of the sand.

A black figure raced like the wind between those sandy shapes. Any hand or body that threatened to block his path was promptly severed, with some of the would-be assailants turning to dust on the ground and others doing so in midair.

Having already covered more than twenty yards at full speed, D artlessly slammed his blade into the right shoulder of yet another foe that stood in his way. True to the strange feel of what it was cutting, the blade hacked halfway through the creature's chest before stopping. As the Hunter pulled his blade free, his foe pounced, turning back into sand over D's head.

Ignoring the sand men that were springing up all around them, D quietly inspected his longsword. Black grains clung to the blade—

iron dust—causing his weapon to lose its edge. If it stuck to steel it had a powerful magnetic charge, and that had to be what helped the sand men keep their humanoid shape. But understanding the reason did nothing to help the irrefutable fact that D's offensive might had dropped considerably.

Sand creatures were packed all around them. Tae clung to D's waist while D gazed at his blade without saying a word. It was a cold, clear gaze that seemed to suggest that this young man would greet life and death, joy and sorrow, all with the very same look.

The wind snarled loudly.

As an eerie shudder climbed her spine, Tae saw the sand men stop . . . and then back away immediately. When the girl looked up at D again, she learned the reason: his eyes were giving off a red glow.

D dashed forward, carried by the wind. He landed right into the heart of the sand men. With the coolness of an artist raining destruction on a group of standing sculptures, the Hunter swung his longsword in wide arcs. His blade was already thick and black with the iron particles that clung to it. As if to demonstrate the power of his Noble blood, he left a few of the sandy monstrosities split from head to crotch, while others were sliced clean through the torso. Without exception, they all returned to their original material. As the wind blew the dust from the crumbling bodies into D's face, his crimson eyes gleamed beautifully and with ineffable mystery.

Someone was shouting in the distance. D leapt into the air and over the edge of a nearby sand dune. Off to his left, the upper body of another sand man stretched from the ground.

Tae was about to scream when right before her very eyes D's left hand snapped closed on the featureless face of a sand man. Dust spilled from between the Hunter's fingers, and the creature's head broke apart like a clod of dirt.

But the sight that greeted them next was like some sort of miracle. The countless sand men crumbled to pieces in a matter of seconds and mixed with the dusty clouds, as if some titanic hand had wiped them all out of existence.

The Dark Forest

CHAPTER 5

I

As the Hunter and the girl returned to the wagon, they were met by Granny's wrath-filled visage. Despite having defeated the sand men by some means even D didn't understand, she didn't seem confident in herself. There would be more trouble related to Tae, it seemed.

"The water's shot," Granny said, pinning Tae with a reproachful gaze as she did so. "Before she ran off on us, the girl left the spigot on the tank open. We've shut it again, but given the number of us, what we have won't last half the day. If we spread it thin as possible, we'd still only get three days."

"If there were only half as many of us, it'd last six days," Clay interjected with amusement from high in the saddle. "Care to see who's gonna get to drink that water?"

The space between all of them was strung with invisible threads of tension.

"You've got a point there," Granny said, looking as she did at Lance from the corner of her eye. "I suppose we can't let those that aren't pulling their own weight drink our water."

Lance lowered his eyes. He was well aware of where he stood.

"How long would it last between four people?"

At that abrupt question, Granny stared at the young man in black with astonishment. "Well," she replied, "barely a day and a half, I suppose."

"Make it two."

"I suppose we can manage that. But traveling by day should be a lot more painful for you than it is for us."

"The night makes up for it. He can have my share."

The old woman turned and exchanged glances with Clay. "Now, this is a surprise. I didn't know you were one to worry about anyone else. And here I thought you had liquid darkness flowing through you instead of blood. That's very kind of you, but me and Tae will take it instead."

But Granny was in for yet another surprise.

Sulkily, Clay said, "I don't want any either."

Not only did Granny have her mouth agape, but Lance did as well.

Gazing steadily at D, Clay said, "If he ain't drinking, there's no way I'm gonna keep wetting my whistle. If anybody could accuse me of taking the easy way out, I'd never live it down."

"Oh, dear me, if that's not enough to bring a tear to my eye," Granny said, bowing her head as if deeply touched. "I've lived a good long time, but I've never heard anything as fine as all that. Yes, indeed—you men can be mighty impressive. Good enough. I'll give both your shares to Tae."

It was just like the crone to make no mention of what would become of her own share of the water. But just then a third shock was delivered to Granny.

"That won't be necessary," the girl declared.

"How's that?" asked Granny.

Everyone turned to the girl, who met them with a distant look in her eyes. She was staring off in the same direction she'd headed during her escape. The fact of the matter was that Tae had someone to guide her.

"What do you make of this?" the old woman said to D.

"Apparently there was no need to bring her back," the Vampire Hunter muttered in a low voice from the back of his horse. A weary shadow hung on his gorgeous countenance. The sunlight and scorching heat of the desert were foes of the highest order for those who descended from the Nobility. Even for the greatest of dhampirs, the physical exhaustion was far more intense than it was for human beings.

Tae leapt down from the driver's seat. Granny reached out for her with one hand, but D stopped the old woman.

"The desert's definitely calling out to the girl," the Hunter said. "Given how it wrecked our water supply, it could be calling us, too."

"What do you suppose it's up to?"

"We'll just have to go see."

"Isn't that dangerous?" asked the old woman.

"There'll be danger no matter where we go."

"Okay. I can't very well let my merchandise run off. I'll follow along right behind. Right behind *you*, that is. Otherwise, you're liable to say none of this is any of your concern and keep right on going."

"Would I?" D muttered, tugging on his reins.

Tae was already walking away. The footprints she left in the sand were pathetically small. As if guided by those tiny tracks, the rest of the party advanced. The moment the girl disappeared behind a massive sand dune, D turned and looked back.

"Worried about the sandstorm?" Granny asked.

Needless to say, she got no reply.

Clay passed his vigilant gaze from left to right. While he was on his guard for sand men, it should've come as little surprise that a mischievous grin lingered on his lips. Even matters of life and death were little more than a game to this warrior.

The group continued for more than three hours. The sun had risen even higher, burning deep black shadows of the party into the sand.

"Say, mister," Lance called out to D from the driver's seat of the wagon, where he'd taken Granny's place. Having cowed him with threats about his share of the water, the crone was now stretched out beside him with the canopy shading her face—her concern for Tae keeping her from going inside. At first, Granny had been quite worried about the girl as she headed off so purposefully, but after seeing the steadiness of Tae's steps, the old woman complied with D's instructions not to interfere. She refrained from calling out to the girl as she walked away, however, anxiety about protecting her merchandise kept her countenance stiff.

"What is it?"

On hearing D's reply, Granny was more surprised than anyone. Having this Hunter actually reply when someone called out to him was like seeing the whole world turned upside down.

"How about you switch with me and come take the driver's seat?" Lance suggested. "It'd be a lot easier on you. There's shade from the sun and everything."

"Don't worry about it," D replied.

"Yeah, but—"

"I'm used to it. Have you ever ridden a horse before?" the Hunter asked.

"A little. I could handle one if it was just walking along like that."

"Your job is to make the wild places green."

"I've lost my faith in doing that," Lance confessed.

"Why?"

Granny had been silently listening to the pair's conversation, but her eyes bugged out then. Anyone who knew D would've had exactly the same reaction. The very thought of D—the great Vampire Hunter D—wanting to know anything about anyone else boggled the mind.

"All you folks have these incredible abilities," Lance replied. "By comparison, I'm just a plain old farmer. I can't do anything but reclaim soil and plant things. And then, when I found myself out here in the middle of the desert, I couldn't even save myself without help from all of you. I'm pathetic. You know, I'm twenty-five now. Do you suppose there's still time for me to become a Hunter?"

D's head didn't turn, but his eyes slid to the side. "What do *you* think?" he said.

Finding himself at the end of D's question, Clay clucked his tongue. "Sheesh. If it was that easy for every sodbuster and his brother to become one, we'd be up to our asses in Hunters. Guys like you should be Vegetable Hunters or Piglet Hunters," he told Lance.

"That might not be bad," the man replied.

"Bah," Clay said, spitting in disgust. "You're completely hopeless. You could die out here and I bet there ain't a single soul who'd miss you."

"You're right. My mother and father were both carried off by a flood."

Sitting there beside Lance, Granny donned an expression that seemed to say, "Heaven help us."

"What sort of things did you plan on planting?" asked D.

"Anything. If it'll grow with fresh air and water and sunshine, then anything at all."

"Well, that's what you should do."

"Damn straight. That sort of shit suits you," Clay said spitefully.

"It's a job we can't do," D remarked, putting a sullen look on the younger Bullow's face. "I can swing a sword, but I don't know how to plant seeds. I can kill Nobles, but I can't raise a single vegetable. There wouldn't be a problem if all the Hunters were gone, but people can't live without food."

"Maybe in theory that's true . . ." Lance conceded. "But a Hunter gets some appreciation when he takes care of something, right? No matter how much of the earth we've made green, no one has ever thanked us for it. Yeah, I sure wish I could use a sword a bit more like a dhampir."

His envious remark was rocked from the air by an explosion of laughter.

"What's so funny?!" asked Lance.

Holding her belly, Granny said, "How could you *not* laugh at that? You're the only person I ever met who wanted to be a dhampir. I get it now. Seems farmers don't know a whole lot about the world. You'd best stick to planting seeds for the rest of your days."

"What's so funny about dhampirs? That's a pretty good thing to be, isn't it?"

"Take a good look at our young friend here," Granny said, staring at D with a fierce look in her eye. Her gaze seemed to harbor what could be taken for hate, which surprised Clay as well as Lance. "Absolutely perfect from head to toe," she continued. "What more could you ask for? Any woman—any man, for that matter—can take just one look at him and get lightheaded. But he treads a path that's painful as hell."

Lance didn't know what to say.

"Tell me," the old woman said, "have you ever fished off a river-bank? Fun, isn't it? I'm sure you've picked flowers and seen sunlight sparkling in the breeze, too. Everyone does those things, but he can't. Sunlight burns his flesh like a blowtorch. If he fell into running water, he couldn't even move his limbs properly. Touch a rose, and he'd scream and wither away. A gentle breeze? If it blew against him, it'd rip the skin and muscle from his bones. Did you say something about people appreciating dhampirs?" Granny asked. "Let me give you some facts about just what sort of rigmarole goes on when one of them comes to work for a village. For starters, while the dhampir is there, no women or children are allowed to leave their houses at all. In cases where it's really bad, they're all locked up in one spot and don't come out again until business is taken care of. Any hand or foot that comes into contact with the dhampir gets scrubbed and disinfected until the skin comes right off it, and in the case of livestock, the animals are put down on the spot. That much they could stand. But the whole time they're in a given village, not a single person will ever look them in the face . . . and that's hard to do."

The words came like flames from the crone, but D listened without comment. Stunned by this bombshell, Lance and Clay both gazed at the woman's wrinkled face in disbelief.

As if she'd just noticed them, Granny snapped back to her usual self. "Goodness me," she said, pressing her hand to her mouth as if she'd just told a joke. "That was terribly rude of me. Let's just pretend I didn't say any of that. Okay, everyone? Is that all right, D? Don't make such a stern face," she told the Hunter. "Oh, I'm sorry," she added, "That's the way you always look, isn't it? Well, at any rate, tell me you don't hold it against me."

The Hunter said nothing.

"Oh, come now. You can't take the hysteric outburst of an old lady that seriously. Please. Just say this one thing for me. Tell me you don't hold it against me."

"It didn't bother me," said D.

"Don't tell me it didn't bother you; say you don't hold it against me. As a special favor to an old woman."

"I don't hold it against you."

"Thank you kindly," the old woman exclaimed, breaking into a grin as she raised one hand in thanks.

Wearing a look that absolutely defied description, Lance gazed at D.

"I guess dhampirs got it pretty hard, too," said Clay, who sounded unusually introspective.

Ahead of them, a few low mountains of sand appeared. They were perhaps twenty feet high or more, but the inclines were gentle. Tae began climbing them with a regular gait. Granny switched her wagon into low gear.

Tae and D were the first to reach the summit; next came Granny's wagon. Then Clay galloped up last. All halted there. There was no wind to welcome them.

"I see," Granny said, sounding deeply impressed. "I suppose that'd make anyone want to give up farming."

About two hundred yards off, the desert underwent a remarkable transformation. No trace remained of the boundless sea of sand.

Lush green filled everyone's field of view, and it stretched off without end to either side. The scent of cool ozone tickled the nostrils of all. The towering trees seemed to reach heights of easily four hundred feet. The desert had chosen to greet the party with a massive forest.

II

Though they all recalled what this had to be, it was Granny that said its name. "So, this is the moving forest—it has to be a trap, right?"

"More than likely," the Hunter replied. "But at least we should be able to find water here."

"It's a damn good trick. Never seen an oasis like this before," Clay said, his eyes sparkling with admiration. But this was no mere oasis. It was a vast forest the likes of which couldn't be found even in the heavily wooded regions of the north. The vista was more than just magical . . . it was close to miraculous.

"What do we do, eh?" the crone asked.

"Unless we want to roast here, we have no choice but to go on. We have a guide," D said, turning his gaze to Tae, who'd stopped a few yards ahead of him.

"You have to do something for her," Granny said. "If you don't wake her up fast, she'll wind up serving the desert for the rest of her life."

"There's nothing we can do for her at the moment. We'll have to take the desert itself out of action. For the time being, our hands are tied."

"Hmph!" the old woman snorted. "Here you are, a dhampir, and you're completely useless."

"At any rate, let's go," Clay said, raking the fingers of one hand through his hair. Grains of sand rained noisily to the ground. "This trip's just about bored the hell out of me. I need me a bit of stimulation, I think."

No one had any objections, and there was little else they could do. Tae began walking again. With nothing to stop them, the party followed along after her into the vast forest. As they entered the shade, cool air swept over every inch of them. They suddenly stopped sweating. Granny shivered.

Tae continued between the boles and their endless verdant riot, her steps free from trepidation. It was obvious she was under someone else's control. The only sound the party heard was that of grass and dirt under hooves—absent were the songs of the birds and the chirping of the insects. Apparently, nothing lived in this forest save the trees.

"Hey, sodbuster," Clay called out. "This is a hell of a place we find ourselves. You happen to know what kind of trees these are?"

"Pretty much."

"Well, I feel so much better then," the warrior said, his explosion of laughter coursing out between the trees and then disappearing. But Clay soon clammed up.

"This is a psi attack, right?" Granny asked.

"No," D replied, never taking his eyes off Tae. "This is the real thing. But it's definitely under the desert's control."

"What in the blue blazes does it want with us anyway?" Granny said irritably, and then she quickly looked up.

Lance, who'd been straining his ears, had clapped his hands together. "That sounds like . . . water!" he exclaimed.

"Seems this confounded desert might be good for something after all," said the old woman.

"Only because it has to keep us alive," D remarked.

"With that kind of thinking, you're not cut out for anything but Hunting."

D looked up. The colossal branches overlapped above them, forming a dense canopy. The reason it remained bright despite the fact that sunlight couldn't get through was because bioluminescent fungi clung to the bark of the trees.

"There's something out there," Clay muttered.

"You're right," Granny said. "I can feel it. There are a lot of them, too. I just can't tell where they're coming from."

"I'm sure we'll know soon enough," Clay said, putting his right hand on his harp.

After they'd gone on for five minutes, the sound of water was even more obvious to their ears. Another ten minutes passed, and suddenly a waterfall and pool appeared before them. The silvery ribbon of water dropped straight down from a height of thirty or forty feet.

"This is nice! I'm gonna have me a swim."

But just as Clay made that carefree remark, Tae thudded to her knees ahead of them. Strength draining from her body, she collapsed on her side.

Leaping down from her vehicle, Granny raced over to the girl.

"Is she okay?" Lance asked as he jumped to the ground, too.

D and Clay alone gazed at the dark blue waters that reflected the greenery.

"Doesn't seem to be anything here," Clay said after a while.

Without a word, D rode his horse over to the edge of the lagoon. He didn't so much as glance at Tae or the other two with her. His left index finger went to his mouth. When it quickly came away again, a bright red bead welled from the tip of it. Turning his finger toward the ground, he pressed his thumb against it right next to the bloody bead. A drop of scarlet fell between the waves lapping at the shore, and then vanished in the blink of an eye. Watching the placid surface for a while, D then said, "Looks like you can swim here."

Choosing a flat spot near the water, the group set up camp. By the time Lance finished taking care of the water tank, it was evening. But that only applied to the world outside the forest—D and his companions were still surrounded by the glow of the luminescent fungi.

"That looks like the end of our water woes," Granny said with a satisfied nod when she returned to the driver's seat from an inspection of the tank.

Sitting by the campfire gobbling down the contents of a can of food, Clay remarked, "Sure, but the long and short of it is, we ain't getting out of here till we put this desert down once and for all. We gotta do something fast. Where's the thing's heart, anyway?"

"If we knew that, we wouldn't be busting our humps," Granny replied in a bitter tone as she glanced out of the corner of her eye at D, who reclined against a rock some ten or so feet away.

"What'd you do with Tae?" Clay asked as he looked all around.

"She's in the wagon with Lance."

"Again? You're playing with fire there."

"You needn't trouble yourself about it. I'm sure he won't let his guard down this time."

"I'll take the next shift from him," said the warrior.

"Let the wolf watch the sheep? Don't make me laugh."

"A wolf, am I? That guy's a hundred times more dangerous than me," Clay shot back, his eyes creeping over to D in the shade of a rock.

"That one's had a different upbringing from you. Got a better character, too."

"He's a dhampir. He's bound to get thirsty for blood sooner or later."

"If he does, I suppose I'll just have to chalk it up to bad luck," Granny replied.

"Have it your way then," the warrior said. Clay then hit the outer wall of the wagon with his ridiculously large fist. "Hey! Come out here a minute. I gotta have a word with you."

Both Lance and Tae stuck their heads out.

"My business is with the man of the wagon," Clay said. "I thought we could take a little stroll and chew the fat."

"What, with me?" Lance asked, his eyes wide.

"You got a problem with that?"

"No."

"Then leave the dhampir to watch the women and come with me."

"Don't you hurt him," Tae cried. "He was only looking after me."

"Relax, missy. I might not look it, but in warrior circles, I'm known as something of a gentleman," Clay said with a smirk as he tossed his jaw in Lance's direction.

"D! Granny! Stop him!"

"Let 'em be," Granny said with a wink. "When men get to quarreling, this is the only way to put an end to it. Now you stop for a minute and think about what it means if a couple of boys are ready to throw down over you. And once you're done doing that, get back to your sewing."

"D," Tae called out, her last hope bound to his name. But then she realized that her expectation wouldn't be met. There was no sign of the gorgeous youth in black anywhere.

"He's probably off checking out the area," remarked the old woman.

Now down on the ground, Tae could be heard to say, "I . . . I'll go look for him!"

"Now, just hold on!" Granny cried at the slender back of the girl dashing off toward the rocks. The crone reached for the jar on her hip, but stopped in mid-motion. "Ah, to blazes with it!" she said to herself. "She's at that age, after all." And then she turned to the two men with great dissatisfaction and said, "Unless the two of you are trying to see who can be the world's biggest idiot, you'll knock this off right now."

Going to the side of the rock, Tae looked toward the forest. Between the green leaves, a figure in black could be seen in the distance.

"Wait!" she cried out, and just as she did, the black shape melted into the forest. Before she could even think about turning back, her body was moving forward. As she ran, she called out, "D!"

Stopping where D had disappeared, she looked all around. Twenty or thirty feet off to her left there was a section of open ground, and D stood in the center of the nearly circular clearing.

"D!" the girl cried out. She was about to dash over to him when a low command sharp as a blade stopped her.

"Hide."

Frantically, the girl ducked behind a tree. D had become a statue. Though she strained her eyes, Tae could see nothing around them; perhaps only D knew what it was. At just that moment, something black bobbed up over D's head. Looking at it from a logical standpoint, the object dropping from above with incredible speed had probably slowed its descent at the end to lessen the shock of impact, but to Tae it seemed to just pop up instead. The slight glint the girl saw was like a blow to her heart.

"D!"

The flash of silver that flew up from the ground forced the girl's cry back down her throat. Cut in half around its middle, the dark figure thudded to the ground at D's feet. It was a stark-naked human. However, the hands that grasped something metallic and the legs were abnormally long, reminiscent of a spider. As similar forms dropped from above one after another, Tae gasped.

D's longsword flashed out, and those it touched fell to the ground dead. A trio of figures that'd landed out of reach of the blade took to the air. They had incredible leaping power, but that was all they had a chance to show. Without time to use the weapons they had in their hands, they were split in half by the arc of the longsword. D moved lightly. A bloody mist billowed toward him, skimming by his body before it hit the ground.

At some point, enough spider people had descended that their milling shapes blotted out the darkness. If they came at D en masse, even he wouldn't be able to stop all of them at the same time. Perhaps realizing as much, the figures creeping across the ground crouched as one. Before they could advance, they stopped suddenly. A horrifying aura had paralyzed them all—an aura which emanated from D.

"Heading back?" Tae heard the Hunter ask in the same steely tone as always.

The spiders scurried into action. They seemed relieved. For some reason, Tae felt relieved, too.

The bodies of the spider people floated up into the air. Although Tae's eyes couldn't detect what supported them, they rubbed their hands and feet together as they vanished into the treetops. No doubt the reason they seemed to be moving in slow motion compared to their earlier descent was because D's aura had seeped into their marrow.

Suddenly, Tae realized that the two of them were alone.

Turning to her, D asked, "Why did you come here?"

At a loss for words, Tae then remembered what her original motivation had been. "Er . . . Mr. Clay and Mr. Lance are about to . . . " Her voice petered out. She'd just realized D didn't have a whit of interest in that. What became of his fellow travelers was no concern of his. "How can you be so cold . . .?" she said, the words creeping from her mouth unbidden. She had to wonder what her face looked like as she stared at D. She'd tried to regain some composure, but one after another the emotions seeping from her heart became words. "You don't care at all what happens to anyone else, do you? You're nothing but darkness and ice to the very core. No matter what anyone else thinks of you, you can just ignore them like some little puff of wind. I've heard that dhampirs have human blood mixed in with the Noble, but that's a lie. You've got nothing but the cold, dark blood of the Nobility flowing in your veins!" she shouted.

As Tae shouted at him, she shook. It felt like the blood was coursing through her body in reverse, and that it was going to freeze—from fear. No matter who or what they might be, anyone who crossed this youth would be cut down. Tae realized for the first time what this Vampire Hunter *really* was. However, another emotion had welled up with her fright, and it was on this that Tae's consciousness became fixed. The feeling became a sob, and Tae spun around. If nothing else, she wanted to at least keep him from seeing her cry. Leaning back against a nearby bole, Tae sobbed.

"What happened in Castle Gradinia?" the Hunter asked.

The girl heard his voice, but didn't sense him drawing any closer. "Don't come near me," she said. "Just go back. Leave me alone."

"This is dangerous territory. Those things I just fought haven't given up yet. Cry as much as you need to, then I'll take you back with me."

"Stupid Hunter," Tae cried as she turned around. A powerful wall of black blocked her way. "Stupid, stupid, stupid!" Repeating the word over and over all the while, Tae pounded him with her fists. It felt like she was hitting solid rock. "I thought you might be okay. I was so happy, because a man like you could be a dhampir."

"Which of the Nobles fathered the child you carry?"

Tae stopped what she was doing. She thought her blood would freeze, and that even her heart might stop. The girl tried to shut her eyes, but her eyelids wouldn't budge at all. Words alone came to her with usual ease as she said, "What are you talking about?"

"You're pregnant. Which of the Nobles is the father?"

Tae couldn't feel anything anymore. "I don't know," she replied. "Is it *his*?"

That was all he had to say for Tae to understand. Out of the darkness, eyes that were fiery red points of light drew closer.

"Is it *his*?" D asked once more.

"I couldn't help it, you know," Tae said. The girl thought she sounded like an old lady. "What could I do? Either of them could've killed me with just one finger. I had no choice but to do as they told me."

"When did you realize it?"

"Back when I was still in the castle. Do you know what month it'll be born? Ordinarily, it's supposed to take ten months and ten days for a baby."

"Yes, ordinarily. In the case of this child, it'll be about six months after you noticed the first indications."

As if to distance herself from something unseen, Tae took a step backwards. "What do you mean, 'in the case of this child'?"

"If it's *his* child, your baby will be no ordinary dhampir."

"What are you trying to say?"

"Let's go back."

"No. Tell me. What'll my baby be like? It couldn't be," Tae mumbled. "It couldn't be . . ." The second time she said it, she tried to invest the words with nothing but horror. But something had welled up inside her. Although she wasn't even aware of it, Tae was now hopelessly in its power, under the sway of a sad yet mysterious delight. "Just like you . . ." she continued.

Something cold touched her cheek. Before Tae realized it was D's left hand, her consciousness had become one with the darkness.

"An awful tale it is, but interesting still," D's left hand muttered as it caught the collapsing girl. "I wonder what road the girl will take? Anyway, those characters you faced just now have been keeping tabs on you ever since you were down by the water. That's why you drew them out here, isn't it?"

"That was a test, I imagine. For me."

"Testing your abilities? What for?" asked the voice.

"Don't you know?"

"Nope," the voice said, its reply vested with laughter. Malicious laughter. "Come now. You know just as well as I do. This desert has a real nostalgic feel to it."

D put Tae over his left shoulder.

"Just when and how did things get so crazy?" the voice continued. "I remember something a woman we met once said. She wanted to know why something so good had to end so badly."

"Do you think this is something good?" the Hunter asked.

"I don't know."

D started to walk back. And the voice wasn't heard again.

III

By the time D came back with Tae over his shoulder, the fight between Clay and Lance had ended. Lance lay stretched out by the edge of the lagoon, spread-eagle. His face was swollen to nearly twice its normal size, and his nose was a bit crooked.

Detecting the Hunter as she washed out a cooling cloth, Granny raced over to him.

"She's fine. I just put her to sleep. She'll come around in about ten minutes," the Hunter said. A light flip of his black shoulder put Tae's body into the air, and an agitated Granny caught her. Taking a quick glance at Lance, D remarked, "He won, didn't he?"

"I'm surprised you could tell," Granny said with a grin. "That fool Clay is laid out in the bushes over yonder. The farmer gave it to him pretty good. But Clay's not all bad, either. He fought bare-handed to the very end."

"Get everyone into the wagon. I'll stand watch," D said, his eyes on the flow of the waterfall all the while.

"You mean those two yahoos, too?"

"You can have them sleep outside if you like," D told the old woman.

"I'll do just that. Good luck with the guard duty."

As Granny carried Tae in both arms and walked unsteadily toward the wagon, Lance got up. His face was a mess. "Is she okay?" he asked.

"You needn't concern yourself with her, you useless thug. The nerve of you, going off like you're something special and getting your good-for-nothing face beat purple in a fistfight. And just so you know, I won't hear of you asking me for the day off tomorrow," Granny snarled.

Even after the old woman had vanished into the wagon with Tae, her ill-tempered remarks still hung in the air.

"It seems you beat him," the Hunter commented.

Raising his head, Lance looked at D with a strange expression on his face. He couldn't believe the young man would bother to say that to him. "Back in the old days, I was a little hellion," he said. "Besides, you can't beat a farmer barehanded. Hunters and warriors came to my village a lot, and they taught me some fighting moves, too."

"Sounds like he bit off more than he could chew," D said as he turned toward the bushes Granny had mentioned. The head of a shadowy figure was listlessly rising from them. "Was this about the girl?" D asked Lance.

"Yeah."

"You really went at it, didn't you?"

"I didn't have a choice. I couldn't just stand there and let him beat the hell out of me."

"Well, that may be a bit of welcome news," said D.

"For who?"

"There're not a lot of men who'd get their face blown up to twice its normal size for someone else. I bet the girl's never met anyone like that before. I'll tell her what happened."

"Don't bother. That's not what I had in mind," Lance said, sighing.

An arm sheathed in black was offered to the young farmer, making his eyes go wide. Grabbing it by the wrist, Lance pulled himself upright.

"So there you are, you lousy sodbuster!" Clay roared, his massive body being carried closer by an uncertain gait. When his face came into the light, it was nearly twice as swollen as Lance's. "What do you say to a rematch? I ain't taking no for an answer."

"Maybe later," Lance said, smiling for some reason.

"Shut your hole!" Clay bellowed, and he was about to grab hold of the smaller man when an arm in black restrained him. "What do you think you're doing?! Let go of me!" he shouted at the Hunter.

"Let him go, D," Lance said as he rubbed the back of his neck to loosen it up. "I thought I'd settled this once and for all, but if he hasn't given up yet, there's not much else I can do. Okay," he told Clay, "now swear to me again that if I win, you'll stay the hell away from the girl."

"No problem, and Vampire Hunter D is my witness."

The figure in black stepped away from them.

Shouting something, Clay took a swing at Lance. The warrior was stumbling over his own feet.

After ducking the blow, once Lance heard it whistle through the air above him, he rammed himself headfirst into Clay's stomach.

Ouf! With a howl more akin to an explosion, the warrior's massive form flew into the air with ease, and Clay landed on his back in the same spot by the water where Lance had been lying. The ground rumbled.

Leaping into the air, Lance slammed his elbow down on his opponent's solar plexus with the full weight of his body. Something resembling water sprayed from Clay's mouth; his body shuddered, and the battle was over.

"There won't be any more rematches."

Lance nodded at D's remark. Clay didn't move a muscle.

Getting to his feet, Lance looked down at his vanquished foe. In a matter of seconds, the same grin he'd worn moments earlier covered his face again. For although Clay's fierce countenance was contorted with pain, it was also etched with an undeniable smile.

Two hours passed.

Even the activities of the fungi might've been governed by biorhythms, for a deep blue filled the darkness and enveloped the party by the water's edge.

D set his saddle down by the campfire and rested his head on it as he reclined there. The men with the badly swollen faces lay covered by blankets a few yards away. Had the moon been out that night, it was so silent that they would've heard its beams raining down.

D mentioned the incident with the spider people to no one. His eyes were shut. The Hunter might have considered himself to be the only one they were after, or perhaps he was confident that if they attacked him there he could carve his way through them. Whatever the case, as his gorgeous form lay at rest, there was no hint of tension about him.

The wagon's door opened without a sound and Granny peered out from the driver's seat. She was about to say something to D down on the ground below when a rusty voice beat her to the punch.

"Get some sleep." Most likely, the Hunter had caught some otherwise imperceptible creak from the door.

"Well, I can't," Granny said, wearily muttering encouragement to herself as she hobbled down from the wagon and headed over to D rather nonchalantly. The jar on her hip swayed back and forth. Though she gave the impression of being fiercer and more determined than the average old lady, seeing the way she walked just then with her wrinkled cheeks and bleary eyes was like catching a glimpse of some gorgeous dancing girl's true face laid bare when the makeup comes off back in her dressing room. Surely there were nights when the crone felt an acute longing to open that fabric store.

Circling around behind D's back, she took a seat. "Have some?" she asked, thrusting a jug of liquor at his refined countenance. It was the cheap sort of fruit spirits that could be found in great quantities at the general store in any post town.

"No."

Curt as D's reply was, it was odd that it didn't seem at all intended to offend the listener.

"Oh, that's right. I must've mistaken you for someone else," Granny said. Pulling out the cork, she took a swig. Three times her throat bobbed, and after pulling the jug away, the crone wiped her lips with the back of her hand. A long sigh escaped her. "About some of the things that were said to you today—don't take it personally. And I don't just mean what I said. From what I hear, Tae had some pretty harsh things to say too, right? Well, I'd like to make up for that. Kindly accept my apologies."

"Don't worry about it."

"Honestly?" Granny said, breaking into a broad grin like a little kid. "Ah, I'm glad to hear you say that. I didn't think you were a petty man or anything, but it's still a relief. We've got a long ways to go yet. And we really are counting on you."

"You should get some sleep."

"Stop trying to get rid of me," the old woman replied. Wrapping both hands around her knees, Granny watched the endless ripples on the water's surface. "You know, don't you?" she said after some time passed. "You know about the girl—that she's pregnant. And that it's probably a Noble's baby. If someone doesn't fix it, she'll be having that kid sooner or later."

Saying nothing, D continued to lie there with his eyes closed. As to what sort of thoughts passed through his mind, no one could say. "What'll you do?" D then asked, muttering the question.

"What's this? You're actually interested in someone else's fate? I'll take her home, of course. That's my job, after all."

"In that case, you didn't need to bring it up at all."

"Well, there are times I just feel like doing or saying something funny. I bet you get the urge sometimes to just lie out in the sun and get a tan."

"She's not going to be very welcome, even back at her own home," D said, returning to the topic of Tae. "Especially not if she's going to have a Noble's baby. And she won't be able to hide that. It doesn't matter how strong anyone says she is; strength probably won't be enough to resolve this problem."

"You trying to tell me not to take her back?" Granny said in a tone charged with defiance. "Because that's the one thing I simply can't do. I've said it before, and I'll say it again—this is my job. No matter what happens later, everyone's overjoyed at first, and there's coin in it for me. What comes next—well, forget it. I'd just be repeating myself. You've already heard my spiel on the matter, and hearing it again ain't gonna make it any more interesting."

"How's her sewing?"

"She seems to have a real knack for it. She was rattling away at it earlier, too. Not that I have a clue what she's making," the old woman said. "So, what do you suppose will happen with her kid? It'll be a dhampir, won't it?"

"If it's a Noble's child."

"I was wondering if maybe you couldn't look after it . . . you being a fellow dhampir and all. You could teach it all it needs to know from the very start. I mean, you're Vampire Hunter D, after all. It's not like you couldn't afford to feed a girl and her baby. I'm sure you of all people could find some way of making a living besides being a Hunter, couldn't you?"

"Is that what you think?" D asked.

"Yes, indeed."

"Then why am I still a Hunter?"

Granny nodded gravely, as if she'd been waiting for him to say that. "Because you're too awkward. Your pride won't allow you to mix with normal people and live the slow life. That Noble blood is tricky stuff. No matter how you might bend your principles or how much you might try to accommodate the world, you couldn't allow yourself to do that. I suppose it'd take, say, a hundred years before you'd settle into it."

"Why a hundred years?"

"What I mean to say is, if they tried at it hard enough for that long, even a Noble could wind up being agreeable to their situation. Of course, I'm not sure there'd be any guarantees where you're concerned."

"Why do you think that?"

Granny gazed at D intently. "You're out looking for something." She said this casually enough, but the words were tough as steel. "People are always making a big deal about 'Hunters this' and 'Hunters that,' but if you ask me, they're all just a bunch of muscle-bound social misfits. There's only one thing any of 'em care about—being good at killing. When it comes to the worst of the lot, the killing is the whole point of it. Some have wound up plying their skills on upstanding folks; others have been killed by fellow Hunters. Take a peek into their dreams sometime. They're all either pitch black or blood red. And out of the lot of them, there's only one word you'll never find in their heads. I'm sure you know what that is?"

"I don't know. What?"

"'Tomorrow,'" Granny said with quiet confidence. "But you have it in you. Heck, it doesn't even matter whether you think you do or not. And it doesn't even have to be the word *tomorrow* . . . it could be *dream* or hope or *rainbow* . . . or even *love*. Don't laugh. I tell you, there's a huge difference between those who're looking for something, and those who've never had it. But in your case, I get the feeling it's something altogether different."

"What do you think it is?" D asked.

"I don't know. I can't even imagine what it'd be. But you're searching for something, nonetheless. And I bet you could tell Tae's baby all about it someday, too."

The Hunter said nothing.

"You should do that. Shoot, once I've brought her home, it's no skin off my nose. Run off with her if you like. There's a girl who'd be tough enough for a life of one road trip after another. And if she wanted to settle down when the kid got older, you could go back out on the road alone. After you've seen to it that the little one has a proper 'education,' of course."

"Sorry to say it, but there's someone else far better for the job."

"Huh?" Granny said, knitting her brow as she turned around. Under a lumpy pile of blankets some way off, Lance was staring at them. "Spare me. You think a plain old farmer's cut out to handle a dhampir? I can just imagine him trying to run away in the dead of night if it went after him. Even a dhampir's real parents can't hold back its Noble blood."

While it wasn't immediately clear if he'd caught the crone's remarks of bald-faced contempt, Lance got out of his blankets and lethargically made his way over to the campfire. "I heard your conversation," he said as he gazed at the flames.

"Well, you shouldn't have," Granny said angrily. "D, you knew he was awake and you still let him listen in, didn't you?"

Of course, D kept his silence.

"I don't know about all that stuff," Lance said in a weary tone. "But I've got a feeling I'm up to it."

"Up to what?" Granny asked, her face growing pale.

"Well, you know—making a life with the girl," Lance replied, flushing madly.

"Sonny, you must still be talking in your sleep. You, a lousy little farmer of all things."

"What does the girl's family do?" D asked.

"They're farmers," Granny said, somewhat crestfallen.

"Then it doesn't sound like an odd match at all."

"That's right," Lance agreed. "Leave the baby to me. I'll help the kid find the life that suits him best."

"The world's not as simple as all that," Granny declared. "For the most part, dhampir men and women are gorgeous. As babies or even small children, they're goddamn cherubs. Heck, there's plenty of folks who'll try to get close to someone they know is a dhampir. But sooner or later, when that Noble blood shows itself the ones who buttered them up with all that sweet talk are the first ones to take to their heels. And what the blazes are those they leave behind supposed to do, eh? You'll do the same. I'm sure of it. So, stop trying to be so glib."

"That's telling him, you old hag!" another voice added nastily.

Lance and Granny turned to see Clay coming toward them.

With his hatred-filled eyes fixed on Lance, he added, "She's a lot more than a lousy sodbuster like you deserves. Before this trip's over, you'll be dead anyway. Then anybody who wants to can woo her."

"And you think you can win her heart?" Granny asked, glaring at Clay with her hard gaze until he looked away. "You might want to consult a mirror," she sneered. Granny's eyes then shifted to Clay's hip. "Say, does that weapon of yours have any use besides killing?" she asked.

"You're joking, right?" the warrior snarled back like a beast. His right hand skimmed by his hip, and an elegant note resounded. Apparently, the weapon could also be used precisely as its form suggested. "I got this beauty after killing a Noble," Clay told them. "Found it in his concert hall. Just look at her, would you? The strings are silver and the body's gold. And she plays music like you never heard before—music that's pure heaven."

"Then play something."

"Excuse me?!"

"Don't give us that sour puss," the crone said. "You've gone and got our attention. Now, why don't you play us a tune that'll tug on our heartstrings? If you can't manage that, a lullaby will do."

Clay snorted angrily. "Right. You're flat out of luck. I don't use it for useless crap like that. This little treasure keeps me alive. You think I'd play it for a bunch of scum like you?"

"Sure you wouldn't play it for *her?*" D said.

Everyone turned toward the wagon then, even Clay. A tiny figure was crouched in the driver's seat. The eyes that looked at her held so many various emotions that Tae had to divert her own gaze from them.

"You'd like to hear a tune, wouldn't you?"

The girl's pale face bobbed sharply in reply to Granny's question.

"Well?" D asked. Astonishingly enough, it almost sounded like he was ribbing the warrior.

Clay remained hesitant.

"Oh, is that how it goes? The Frontier's top warrior turns down a young lady's request? You can kill folks just fine, but can't even make one girl happy—I guess men aren't worth spit these days."

"You'll eat them words!" Clay said in response to Granny's insults. He began grinding his teeth together as his whole body trembled with rage. It wouldn't have been strange if he'd unleashed an explosion of ultrasonic waves just then. "It's really more than your grubby little ears deserve, but I'll play you one of my best songs. Just don't get so swept up by my sweet voice you go and jump in the lagoon or anything."

Granny and Lance cried out with surprise and delight and clapped their hands.

Clay's rough fingers took to the strings. It was as if the white darkness gave birth to the sounds. Granny's smirk disappeared.

The song was about a man and a woman who lived on the Frontier. The man traveled, and the woman chased along after him. And then both the man and the woman grew tired and settled down into their own lives without ever meeting each other. Long, peaceful days stretched by, and then one day the woman suddenly recalled her old love and gave up everything to follow after him.

High and low, Clay's voice flowed along the ground and danced across the sky in a way that made Granny bug her eyes. His voice was so rich, his notes so precise. The warrior had undergone a remarkable transformation into a troubadour.

Having laid the weary heroine to rest in the cold earth, Clay intoned a few words of prayer, and then halted his fingers on the harp.

The very first applause came from the farthest away. As the men gazed silently at the pale and dainty hands the girl was clapping together, they realized she was weeping.

"Damn, you're good!" Granny said in a voice perilously close to tears.

"Damn straight I am, hag! See, sodbuster?" Clay said, glaring around at the others with loathing before puffing his powerful chest out in Tae's direction. "How's that? Pretty great, wasn't it? Unlike a certain Hunter, I got more than just looks going for me. Yeah, I reckon anybody with an eye for men could tell in a flash who's the best around here. How about it, missy? Forget about going back home—oh, that's right! As long as the sodbuster's alive, I ain't supposed to woo you. Well, don't take it too hard."

And having said everything he wanted to say, the younger Bullow went right back to his blanket, pulled it up over his head, and went to sleep.

Turning to each other, Granny and Lance grinned wryly. Even Tae was smiling. Some people could prove useful in the most unexpected ways.

For a long time, no one moved or said anything.

"Why don't you get some sleep?" D finally suggested.

"I believe I will," Granny said as she got up. "You get some shut-eye, too," she told Lance. Her tone was amazingly amicable.

Lance didn't move. Though he kept staring at her, Granny said nothing more to him and climbed up to the driver's seat.

"Head inside now," the old woman told Tae.

The girl didn't move.

Granny's brow furrowed. Fine blue veins bulged to the surface. The crone then let out an exasperated sigh. Shooting Lance a look he wouldn't soon forget, she hunched her back and disappeared into the wagon.

Both hands folded neatly in her lap, Tae sat staring straight ahead. Seating himself by the fire, Lance wrapped both hands around his knees as he gazed straight ahead, too. Tae watching Lance. Lance watching Tae. The pile of logs must've collapsed, because the flames danced wildly and released a flurry of sparks.

As Lance closed one of his hands around the other, they were both trembling a bit. "Um, I . . ." he mumbled. He sounded like someone else entirely. What would come next?

The flames blazed, and Tae patiently gazed at the emaciated young man.

"Stupid bastard . . ." a jet-black voice grumbled from under the blankets.

Clay's hand crept to his harp, and then stopped suddenly. Something slim and white had zipped between his hand and the instrument, pinning his blanket to the ground. Even without seeing the finely honed tip, he knew it was a wooden needle. Rattled to his very bones by anger and horror, Clay then heard the steely voice of the one who'd hurled it.

"Human or dhampir, no one knows what's going to happen."

Lance turned to D in astonishment. In the Hunter's words he'd heard the very thing he'd been struggling to say. *I want to spend my life with you.* An almost heartbreaking decisiveness surfaced on his face, and he headed toward the wagon.

D's eyes thrust open and caught a glimpse of ripples on the water's surface. Black as the darkness, the Hunter jumped up. Something whizzed loudly through the air, and whatever it was then spattered black blood all around him.

A cry of pain arose nearby.

When D looked back, Lance was pinned on the ground with what looked like a black spear protruding from his chest. The body of it stretched back to the lagoon, painting a gentle yet disturbing parabola that sank back into the water at one end. There was no mistaking what it was—a tentacle tipped with steel.

Melody of Destruction

CHAPTER 6

I

"L ance!" two people called out at once. One was Tae, leaping down from the driver's seat. The other was Clay, who threw off a blanket that'd been run through as well.

Several tentacles that'd been severed by D squirmed away, but new ones shot from the water's surface, stretching for the Hunter, Tae, and Clay.

Forgetting her own fear, Tae raced to Lance's side, but the tentacle that had impaled him instantly wrapped around the girl's body. Assailed by the agony of being bound tight with steel cable, Tae could barely scream, let alone breathe. But the second it jerked her toward the lake, a figure in black blew in like a veritable gale and severed the tentacle.

Zing! Zing! Zing! Tentacles continued to tear through the air to attack the group.

"Get in the wagon," D said, lending Lance his shoulder as he gave Tae a shove.

Lance convulsed. The tentacle piercing his chest thrashed fiercely despite the fact that it'd been cut off. The naked blade flashed out once more, slicing off its tip and putting an end to its movements.

"Cover your ears and hit the dirt!" Clay shouted.

For a moment, there was nothing—and then the most exquisite melody filled the night air.

They watched. All of the fiendish limbs whirring through the air broke apart, reduced to shattered fragments, and then faded before they reached the ground. Not only that, but the rocks of the waterfall, the trees on the opposite shore, and even the now-frothy water disappeared, robbed of their molecular bonds.

Perhaps unable to take any more of this, what remained of the tentacles retreated into the water. There would be no further attacks from them.

Clay's harp was truly something to be feared. If the sonic waves of death were only focused in an extremely narrow kill zone and not capable of being directed with an ease that was itself terrifying, then a monster moving as fast as the wind might be able to avoid them. However, the slightest touch by a single finger of the warrior's hand would send the deadly melody out at anything within listening range. Who could possibly defend themselves from ultrasonic waves that fanned out from the instrument, breaking virtually any material down to its constituent atoms?

"What in blazes is it?!" Granny cried as she flew out of the vehicle. Trusting Tae and Lance to the old woman, D hopped onto his horse. Clay followed after him.

"We're getting out of the woods. Follow me."

Leaving only his words behind, D galloped off. The wind snarled in his wake, but a second later, the strangest thing happened. All around them the light rapidly faded. Even the glowing fungi were under the desert's control.

Abandoning the path they'd come by, D shot straight through the forest. Throwing up a cloud of dust, the wagon and Clay followed close behind.

"D, where are we going?" Granny shouted shrilly from the driver's seat.

But the old woman's query was quickly obscured by Clay as he cried, "Here they come!"

When Granny took a peek in her omni-directional safety mirror, her hair stood on end. Once more the surface of the water had grown rough, and tentacles began to rise from its depths. Beyond numbering, together they looked like a single gigantic tree.

Every detail then vanished from sight for all of them. Darkness had claimed the world.

"Dammit! I can't see anything!" Clay howled.

"Tae," Granny shouted, "break out the glow bugs!"

Scant seconds later, a dazzling circle of light gave a bluish glow to the back window of the wagon and its surroundings—yet the light wasn't strong enough to reach D's back as he rode ahead of them.

Could D tell the way out in the pitch blackness? His super-keen dhampir senses could. D had noticed an imperceptible sound coming from above him. He sensed that it was silently descending. Before the spider person had a chance to bring a blade down on D's head, he sliced its torso in two. The Hunter's steel blade cut through the air in an arc, knocking back a number of would-be attackers on either side. They made not a sound, as their deaths were instantaneous.

"They're coming from above us!"

D's words were replaced by the roar of a gun and its fiery trail, and something heavy seemed to be blown off the wagon. There was a repulsive thud near one of the tires, and then an ear-splitting scream arose from the same area.

Tae had her arm out the rear window of the wagon, holding the light-giving glow bugs out to guide Clay, when suddenly long, insect-like fingers grabbed her hand from above. Despite her screams, the fingers tightened their iron grip. The glow bugs fell.

Thunder shook the vehicle's interior. The bullet of iron that had punched through the roof ripped open the spider man's abdomen and hurled him off into the darkness.

"Lance!" Tae cried. Forgetting the pain of her red and swollen hand, she latched onto the young man, who still held a gun in one hand.

His pale face smiling above a blood-soaked torso, Lance asked, "Are you okay?"

"Yes."

"Don't worry . . . I'll always be here . . . to protect you . . ."

"I know you will," Tae replied, tears spilling from her eyes. Just then, she heard a jubilant cry from Granny that sounded miles away.

"There's the way out!"

A pale gray light enveloped the world. D was in the lead, but the wagon was close behind, seeming to pounce like some gigantic animal as it bounded out into the moonlight. The horses' hooves and wagon wheels sank into sand.

"Yahoo! We're out!" Granny exclaimed, smacking the floor of the driver's seat with one hand. Tightly gripping the reins with the other, she prepared to apply the brakes.

"Keep moving!" a low voice urged her, though she had no idea how it drifted all the way back to her from some twenty feet ahead.

"Bu . . . Bu . . . But . . ." the old woman stammered. Before she could finish asking why, an unbelievable scream arose from inside her wagon. "Tae?!"

The door opened and the girl burst out. Her hands and bosom were bright red with fresh blood.

"What's wrong?" the old woman asked.

"It's the forest—the forest!"

"The forest?!" Granny exclaimed, the earth-shattering news shaping her expression.

The forest wasn't shrinking in the distance. Rather, it was getting closer. The whole expanse of trees headed toward them like a wave of epic proportions.

"D, is this another mirage?"

"No. It's real," D said as he rode beside them.

"You don't say," Granny replied with a grin. "In that case, I should be able to deal with it, too."

Shifting the reins to her left hand, the old woman went for the jar on her hip with her right—the source of the same insane power that'd wiped out the sand people in a heartbeat out in the desert.

What sort of picture would the sand from her jar paint?

Knees far apart, Granny pulled her hand back out of the jar. Beautiful colors poured smoothly from her tightly balled fist before spreading across the floor of the wagon. Granny gave a series of small shakes to her hand. But just what sort of unearthly rite were her five fingers working as they held that sand? Flowing steady and unbroken like a thread, the sand seemed unaffected by the motion of the vehicle, or else it incorporated the jolts into its design. Though somewhat fuzzy, the image that formed at the crone's feet was clearly something that existed in this world. It was, in fact, the very forest that was coming up behind them now.

Granny's hand halted. The picture was complete. Now all she had to do was—

It was at that moment that the door behind her opened.

"Mrs. Viper—" Tae said, her face pale. "Clay's been left back in the woods!"

Granny whipped around. "How the blazes did that happen?"

"I, um . . . I dropped the glow bugs. Then after a while, I couldn't hear him behind us anymore . . ."

"Damnation!" Granny growled, grinding her teeth together.

The edge of the forest was following less than twenty yards behind them.

"That bastard Clay. Do you suppose he's dead?" Granny shouted to D.

"I don't know."

"He's dead. I'm sure of it."

"No," D said with a look over his shoulder.

Following his lead, Granny stopped breathing. Perhaps she caught the faintest of sounds.

A black spot suddenly appeared in the otherwise unbroken wall of tree trunks, and from it bounded a figure on horseback. Wildly kicking up sand, the rider chased along after them.

Now out in the moonlight, Clay was licking his lips. And then suddenly the warrior's body lurched wildly forward. His horse had caught its leg on something! As the beast nosed into the ground with a great cloud of dust, Clay sailed over its head, curling himself up in a ball. Amazingly, he landed on his feet when he hit the ground. The way he straightened smoothly from the landing was superbly acrobatic. However, instead of lauding his feat, the forest behind him merely continued its silent advance.

There was no time to make a dash for his cyborg horse. Clay's right hand grasped his harp, but no matter how far and wide the deadly sounds could fly from his weapon, the warrior was up against a vast forest that was miles across. The strings twanged. The number of trees that disappeared must've been in the hundreds . . . but that wasn't enough.

Clay watched absentmindedly as the wall of colossal trees loomed over him. But even in the depths of his despair, he managed to hear something running up behind him, as only the greatest of the Frontier's warriors might. Even before he knew for sure it was the low rumble of hoofbeats, he'd launched himself into the air. He had no idea as to the distance or speed of the rider—well-honed instinct was all he had to rely on. But that was enough to put the warrior's massive frame squarely on the back of D's horse after the Hunter's sudden stop and complete change of direction. By the time the shadow of the forest swallowed the spot Clay had previously occupied, the cyborg horse had galloped forty feet ahead.

"Looks like that's another one I owe you," Clay said, baring his teeth. The words had been a groan of pure hatred.

"Save your thanks for Granny."

"How's that?"

"She told me to go save you," said D.

"Sheesh. What an old busybody."

In a matter of seconds, their horse was alongside the wagon.

"The forest is picking up speed," Granny shouted to the two men.

"We can't outrun it," Clay said, gnashing his teeth. A second later, his eyes went wide.

The wagon had engaged its emergency brake. At the same time, D halted as well.

"What the hell do you think you're doing?!" Clay stammered, foam flying from his mouth.

Grinning at him, Granny said, "Just you wait and see. Watch what I can do!"

The weird sand painting at Granny's feet was still completely intact. While it wasn't all that large, Clay could still make it out clearly in the moonlight. Knitting his brow, he looked to the rear—at the vast forest pursuing them. That's what her picture was. The pattern that had emerged on the ground was the moon and a desert and a forest—the very same forest rolling after them to swallow them all.

Clay forgot all about taking flight. No matter how they struggled, victory seemed impossible. In seemingly impossible cases, he'd normally flee without a backward glance. That was the way Clay was. The only way he and his brother had remained alive and famous for so long was by avoiding futile battles. But now Clay was caught in a raging storm of desire to see the old woman work her magic with his own eyes, a desire that suppressed even the strongest of human urges—that of self-preservation.

Without a sound, a mountainous shadow hid the stars. The chain of enormous trees bearing down on them was like some demonic beast. Clay's field of view was far wider than that of an ordinary person, and it now held two spectacles: Granny, and the forest.

The old woman leaned far forward. Her tiny chest swelled to nearly twice its normal size. She'd taken a deep breath. And then, with all the force of a bent fire-dragon bone snapping back into shape, the old woman leaned forward in the driver's seat and violently expelled the breath in her lungs through her pursed lips. Scattering dazzling colors in the moonlight, the sand painting blew away, and a cry of astonishment slipped from Clay's mouth.

Now bending forward from the overwhelming mass of the vast forest behind them, the foremost rank of trees was suddenly touched with a blinding iridescence, and a second later they had utterly vanished, like dust driven before a mighty gale.

All around D and Clay—the latter of whom sat dumbfounded on the back of the Hunter's steed—glittering particles of light drifted down from the sky. While Clay realized they were the grains of sand that Granny had scattered, he didn't even have the strength to hold his hand out to catch some.

The desert lay flat in the moonlight. It all seemed like a dream.

"Oww," Granny moaned, pounding on the small of her back up in the driver's seat. Her voice sounded weary, and her face looked strangely exhausted. "That was a heck of a thing to be doing at my age! Would it be okay if we took a breather, D?"

"Your wagon has an autopilot setting, doesn't it?"

"You're a heartless one, you know that? You want an old lady like me at death's door up here bumping along like no one's business? My wagon's controls aren't really in the best condition, either. Left to its own devices, there's no telling where this thing may end up."

"That forest was just a sample to test our strength. We didn't hurt the desert that badly. It'll attack us again."

Apparently grasping the situation well enough, Granny reluctantly said, "Okay already," and nodded.

Just then, Tae came out of the vehicle. Her eyes were puffy. She looked just like a fairy who'd come bearing ominous tidings.

"What is it?" asked Granny.

"Lance is dead," Tae said in a firm tone.

II

It took less than thirty minutes to make the small mound of sand. As everyone stood in a circle around it, D took a steel pipe that'd been in the wagon and stuck it in the center of the mound.

"Kind of a strange shape for a grave marker, isn't it?" Granny said dubiously.

A little bit above the center, the long metal pole had a shorter piece strapped perpendicularly with cord. No one there noticed the change in D's expression when he took the marker in his hand. Like a shadow of pain, the palm of his hand was seared and bruised in the same shape as the pipes.

"Never seen one like that before," Granny said, her eyes staring off into the distance. "No, that's not entirely true," she added. "A long, long time ago I think I saw one somewhere in a distant land . . . Now, what the blazes was it? A Noble's grave?"

D gave a small but firm shake of his head.

"Well, isn't someone gonna say a prayer for him?" Granny asked with her hands on her hips. "I'm not really good at that myself. Didn't even say one when my husband died. Too gloomy for me. Would somebody else do it?"

"What's it matter?" Clay said, shrugging his shoulders. And then, staring intently at the grave, he added, "The dolt. Went and died before we could have another rematch. You know, five minutes after we leave, no one will even know this is here," he said, spitting in disgust.

Looking at D, Granny said, "I don't suppose there's any chance a dhampir would know a prayer for a funeral either. So, what are we to do?"

"I'll do it," Tae offered.

"Oh, my—I nearly forgot the most important person. That'll be fine. He sure was devoted to you. That'd be the best memorial he could ever hope for," Granny said, and her tone made it clear her heart was in those words.

In truth, they would've been better off sticking to D's earlier plan and leaving immediately. Their first consideration was making it to the edge of the desert as soon as possible, but not one of them mentioned that. D had carried Lance's body from the wagon, and Clay had dug the hole. While they worked, Tae and Granny kept their eyes on the men every second, as if it was the least they could do.

Taking a few steps closer to the grave marker, Tae wrapped her arms around her own shoulders. Her voice was somewhat indistinct.

We hereby commit our beloved
Into the eternal rest of Thy kingdom,
Into the dreams of Thy gentle arms . . .

The verse broke there. Tae squinted her eyes as she tried to remember. Her frail body shook, but no words came out.

"I've forgotten how it goes," Tae said in a hoarse voice. "It's funny. I used to say my prayers every morning without fail when I was back in the Nobles' castle. I wonder why I can't remember it now."

Something glittered on its way down the girl's cheek. Before it had reached her jaw, D's rusty voice continued her prayer.

Neither great nor small are we;
Off into the distance we go, only to be born again,
And thus are we called the far wanderers . . .

Shifting her line of sight, Tae saw the Vampire Hunter through hazy eyes.

No one moved.

The wind and the moonlight alone flowed around them, disturbing the surface of the sandy mound ever so slightly. Sand coursed smoothly down the slopes. Suddenly, the flow of sand became heavier, and various shapes began to rise from the otherwise flat surface.

Though we wander the earth seeking Thee,
No answers are we given,
Naught but shadows do we see in this troubled world . . .

Behind the stationary figures, other forms moved. Like ghosts walking across the bottom of a lake, they swayed to and fro as they approached. Whether the group noticed them or not was unclear. D didn't move. Clay and Granny both kept their positions by the grave. The wind blew a bit of sand from the shoulders of those drawing ever nearer.

D's voice remained as soft as ever.

Yet we know not fear;
The words of silence are known to us,
And as we see the unseen,
We are Thee and Thou art us.
This far wanderer we now commit to Thee.

The moonlight became a blade that danced out. The sand men who challenged D broke apart, each being cleanly bisected, while the others collapsed before a melody strummed beneath the crescent moon.

Silence descended.

"Well, that didn't take them all of thirty seconds!" Granny said as she pushed Tae toward the wagon.

D turned around. Clay did, too.

New figures were being born of the sands.

"This is crazy!" Clay exclaimed in a voice that choked with fear for the first time. The warrior's self-confidence had crumbled; he realized that these new figures were actually just revived versions of the sand men they had just defeated.

Shapes flowed from the sand like water, encircling the party.

"So, the desert is evolving, too," D muttered.

"Time for fun. I'll blast every stinking one of them to smithereens!" Clay shouted, all five of his fingers tugging at the instrument's strings.

"D, someone's coming!" Granny called out as she sat in the driver's seat with one arm extended.

"Bro!" Clay shouted, but he seemed surprised by something as he froze.

Following the younger Bullow's lead, the sand men also watched the rider approaching from beyond the dunes. There was no telling where he'd been or what he'd been doing, but the sleeping man that swayed there on the back of his horse was the very same Bingo as always. Perhaps his outlandish appearance frightened the desert, because the sand men froze in their tracks. But soon enough, several of them headed toward this new foe.

"Damn! Get in the wagon!" Clay shouted. "You'll be wiped out!"

Not understanding what that was supposed to mean, but goaded by the urgency with which he'd bellowed it, Granny and Tae dove into the wagon.

"Shit! It's too late now," Clay clucked, waving both hands at his older brother. "Stop, Bingo! It's me!"

Whether or not the older Bullow heard him was unclear, but a second later, spheres that sparkled like foam on the water issued from Bingo's mouth. While they may have resembled soap bubbles, the effect they had was beyond anyone's wildest imaginings. The bubbles shattered right in front of the sand men shambling toward him. For a short time there was no change at all in the sand men, but seconds later their bodies began to look incredibly blurry, and then they were suddenly gone.

At that moment, D had the weirdest sensation. Somehow, it felt like the moment one awakens from a dream.

Once more, the group stood squarely in the middle of silence.

"Hey, bro . . ." Clay said, his tone as muddled as if he'd just woken up.

Not replying to the cry from his younger brother right away, Bingo was swaying back and forth in the saddle, but his face suddenly jerked up. Looking and sounding refreshed, he said, "So, you're still with them?" And as he stared in D's direction, his eyes were once again filled with the lethargy of the bizarre sleeper.

When Bingo asked if his brother was still with them, it was probably just another way of saying, "Why haven't you killed the Hunter yet?" Judging by the way Clay grew pale, his brother was reproaching him.

Turning his vacant gaze to D, Bingo said, "Seems you folks have been looking after my brother."

D was silent. His longsword remained in its sheath. Perhaps he assumed no enemies would be coming because Bingo had destroyed them all.

"Suppose I could join your merry band?" Bingo said, his face aimed at the ground as he gave a light kick to his horse's flanks. It looked like something a drunk would do. The mount staggered over to the group. Even the sleeper's horse had a funny gait.

"Another unwelcome guest," Granny snorted. At some point, she'd poked her head out over the driver's seat. "Haven't lost your food and water, have you? Because we don't have any to spare."

"My brother don't need food or water," Clay said with a smirk. "He gets them someplace else."

"That's just fine, then. At any rate, what do we do now, D?" asked Granny. "It looks to me like this blasted desert is even stronger than before. At this rate, we'll never get of here."

"We'll finish it off," D said succinctly.

"How?"

"Someone tried something like this on me before. I'll beat this the same way I once did."

"And how was that?"

"The day will break soon," D said as he looked to the sky in what seemed to be the east. "Until it does, we'll head back to the southwest."

"Southwest?" Granny asked, her head cocked to one side. But her eyes soon went wide. "You mean toward that cloud of dust . . . that sandstorm? Tell me you're joking because—"

Before the crone could finish saying there was no way in hell she'd be following suit, Bingo stopped her. "Right on the money," he said in a tone as vast as the universe.

"Did you see it?" D asked.

"You bet," the elder Bullow replied. "And we ought to put this thing down real quick."

Straddling his horse, D said, "Let's go."

"You're a lost cause, you know that? Never listen to a thing anyone says," Granny muttered. "Remind me of my husband. In the end, he took off one day and never did come back."

"Did you try to stop him?" asked D.

"Nope," the old woman replied, slowly shaking her head from side to side as she jerked on the reins.

A few glances fell on the sandy grave—from D, Clay, and the old woman. Right before they disappeared beyond the dunes, the pale blossom of a face peered sadly from the back window of the covered wagon. And then a wind from nowhere in particular carried a cloud of sand that covered the tiny cross and made the deceased a permanent resident of the desert.

III

The light of dawn revealed a high wall of sand that extended thousands of feet into the heavens. Back on the ground, D halted his horse when a spray of grains began to strike his cheeks. The sandstorm was less than a mile away.

"Wait here," the Hunter said as he turned his back on the party.

"I wasn't about to go into that thing," Granny said, a gloomy look in her eyes as she sat in the driver's seat. "Don't know what you'll find there, but I'm sure you'll probably be back safe and sound, right?"

"Wait twelve hours. If I don't come back, use one of your sand paintings to erase the sandstorm. You can do that, can't you?"

Granny looked at D for a second with apparent surprise, and then quickly pursed her lips as if angry. "Sure, and wipe you right out with it." No sooner had she spoken than she grew pale and added, "But you'd better come back. Without you, I don't know how we'd ever get out of this place. If you think it's getting too dangerous, remind yourself you have a duty to protect a weak old woman and a girl and turn yourself right around. We're still counting on you."

"They'll protect you," D said, looking back at the warrior brothers.

The sight of the two grown men straddling a single horse surpassed amusing and went right into disturbing. There was nothing else they could do, however, as Granny refused to let Clay sit up front with her—mainly because she didn't want him anywhere near Tae.

"But what's inside the sandstorm?"

"I don't know," D replied.

"You don't know, but you're going there anyway? Guess us mere mortals just can't figure what goes through a dhampir's mind."

"When we were going to cut through it before, Tae led us off to the forest," D said as he turned toward the sandstorm.

"You know, you're right," Granny said.

"Most likely, it didn't want us going in there."

"Why not?" asked the old woman.

"That's what I'm going to find out."

Without any words of parting, D advanced into the wind on his horse. After the Hunter had gone fifteen or twenty feet, Bingo came chasing after him and pulled up on his right side—apparently he'd left Clay behind. Considering which hand D used to wield his weapon, the warrior could've easily been cut down there and he'd have no one to blame but himself. Was it merely carelessness on his part, or was he confident he wouldn't suffer that fate? And just what was that bizarre talent for disintegrating things he'd displayed the night before?

Bingo hadn't mentioned that he'd be accompanying the Hunter, nor did he even look at D. While they rode along with a scant three feet between them, neither of them seemed to take any notice of the other. In no time at all, a golden veil of sand and dust shut them in. The sun vanished. It was impossible to see more than a yard ahead of them with the naked eye. Yet through that storm the pair of riders silently advanced.

"My kid brother told me what happened," Bingo said in a sleepy tone. "Seems you saved his life twice now. I'd like to thank you for that."

D said nothing.

"It was the desert that was out to get us, wasn't it?"

"That's right," D said in a rare response. "How did you know?"

"I saw it in a dream," Bingo replied, his voice clearly audible despite the whipping winds. "In my dreams, I saw the desert's dreams. You know, that's where our true intentions come out."

"How about my dreams?" the Hunter asked.

"I'll have to pass on yours. I don't exactly feel like going crazy at my age."

Just what did the elder Bullow mean by that?

"Doesn't seem like anything's lying in wait for us," Bingo said in a tone that suggested he wasn't bothered by the lack of reaction from D. "And after we took the trouble of riding all this way. I wonder if the desert might've changed its mind? Or does it just know what lies ahead for us?" Bingo said, but the howls of the wind scrubbed away his words.

The two riders then kept silent and let the snarling wind tear at the edges of their clothes as they advanced through the golden dust. And then, before they knew it, a shape darker than the hue of the sands came into view up ahead. Neither of the men seemed bothered by it as they advanced.

The wind sideswiping them seemed to strip away the very same yellow curtain it had raised, as desolate ruins stretched all around the riders. And what a wealth of structures this place boasted—even in the midst of a wicked sandstorm. There were vast streets and intricately carved columns. The scattered remains of mysterious machines—parts of some gigantic mechanism perhaps—stretched on forever, fading into the far reaches of the cloud of dust.

Taking a paved road neither end of which they could see, they crossed a bridge that was on the verge of collapsing. At some point, Bingo let his horse fall a length behind D's. The elder Bullow probably realized which of them knew where he was going.

After traveling down a corridor laced with a spider web of cracks, they suddenly came to a magnificent valley. This land where

merciless dust clouds ran wild now opened a gaping maw, and from what appeared to be the bottomless darkness a resilient object that looked like a conglomeration of massive crystals stretched to the heavens. The girth of the various crystals only increased as they stretched higher. The strange disproportion of these objects indelibly stamped both the purpose and consequences of their creation in what could only be described with a single adjective—disturbing.

From the depths of the earth there spilled a pale light. It was alive.

At the edge of the earth, D gazed in silence at the crystalline mountain. Whatever sort of thoughts D had as he looked out at the scene couldn't be read in his elegant features.

"Is that it?" Bingo called out from ten feet behind the Hunter. "You said you saw it in a dream—was this it?"

"Yep." His reply was gummy with sleep and fatigue. "It had some crazy idea about combining humans and Nobility, of all things. Even after the research center here fell into ruin, the machines kept going, and they let the things they made run loose in the desert. Can't say I blame the thing for wanting to get smarter."

Almost as if in response to Bingo's explanation, the light in the depths of the earth grew stronger.

Long before, forbidden experiments had been conducted in the vast region guarded by the sandstorm. Regardless of what the results might've been, time marched on cruelly, and unbeknownst to anyone the abandoned machinery produced a child beyond anything they could have intended.

What did D think of the desert having a will, or the reason it sought to evolve even further? His gorgeous visage clouded darkly from the incessantly blowing sand and glowed mysteriously with the light rising from deep in the earth.

"What now?" asked Bingo.

Saying nothing, D got off his horse. In his left hand he carried a rolled-up blanket. The wind echoed through the heavens.

Taking a knife from his pocket, he bent over and began digging up the ground.

The actions that followed were most likely beyond the comprehension of Bingo, who watched the Hunter from behind. But then, in this condition there was really no telling whether Bingo was awake or asleep, and perhaps the daydreaming warrior never had any intention of watching D at all.

Once he'd dug up enough earth to fill both arms, D opened the blanket. A bundle of thick, twisted branches spilled out—no doubt procured back in the moving forest. Taking two of the logs in hand, D rubbed them together lightly until they produced flames. Throwing them down on the dirt and adding the remaining wood, D then held his left hand up to the flames. The knife in his right hand flashed across the opposite wrist. Fresh blood gushed out like a torrent, falling on the flames and the dark earth so that a strange black smoke billowed from them.

"Is that enough?" D asked.

"I suppose that will do," a hoarse voice somewhere around D's left wrist replied.

That same hand rose high into the air. And as soon as it did, a howling wind twisted all around the young man in black. Sand and dust dancing wildly, the smoke and flames stretched long and thin and perilously close to snapping. Then, finally, they did snap right off. The flames flowed into a single stream of a color that defied description. The palm of D's outstretched left hand swallowed the stream—not only the flames, but the earth that'd tasted his blood, as well.

Earth, wind, fire, and water—all four elements had been assembled. In less than three seconds the strange suction ended. It seemed to have some significance to D, as he then walked over to the rim of the crack in the earth. His horse whinnied and backed away. Arriving at the edge of the precipitous drop, D pulled out a knife with his left hand.

In his mind, something spoke to him and asked: *Are you going to do it?*

The Hunter drew his left hand back behind his head.

A gleaming sphere poked halfway out of Bingo's mouth.

How I've waited for this day so very long. The whole reason I attacked you was because I thought you might put me to rest.

D stopped moving. The prismatic sphere leisurely approached his head.

"Why don't you put yourself at rest?" the Hunter asked.

I tried, but I could not, even though it was what I wished. The temptation to rise again was simply too great. You must tell me, am I the only one who finds it so?

D bent back at the waist. The globe burst without a trace.

Tell me. Everyone wishes to be something else, don't they? Even when they know that it would involve incredible pain and weariness.

D's knife became a flash of light flying through the air.

Don't they?

The flash of light disappeared, swallowed up by part of the crystal forest.

Without pause, D mounted his horse.

"Is that the end of it?" Bingo inquired in a vague tone.

Giving no reply, D began to slowly ride away. After his mount had taken three steps, what sounded like a sigh could be heard from the hole at his back. Seven steps and one part of the crystals gave off a pale glow. Ten steps and the glow became points of light that collapsed into the crystal with a serene sound. After this, nothing more could be heard. Perhaps that's how ruin was. Thousands and then tens of thousands of cracks raced through the glittering mass. Countless fragments formed, and then collapsed.

The two figures slowly riding away didn't flinch. Needless to say, they didn't look back, either.

Two hours after Granny and Clay looked around in amazement at the suddenly abating sandstorm, D and Bingo returned.

"It's finished, isn't it?" Granny asked. "If it's a regular desert now, we should have no problem. Another two days and we'll be across it. It looks like we'll somehow make our arrival date after all. Well, then, let's get a move on!" the old woman cried, pulling on her reins. Her team of four cyborg horses began tearing up the ground.

"Somebody up there must like that guy," Clay grumbled as he climbed on the horse behind his older brother. "Of course, since he had you with him, bro, there was never any question he'd be okay." Only after he'd said it did he seem to realize the contradiction in that logic; he could do no more than don an odd expression.

D rode by the brothers and asked, "Why did you stop what you were doing back there?"

His question dwindled in the distance, but in the end, Bingo never replied.

Three days later, in the early morning, the party entered the town of Barnabas.

"Well, this is where we say our goodbyes. Really, the only reason we made it this far was thanks to all of you. I could thank you a million times. Hey, you come out here, too," the absurdly jubilant Granny called back to Tae from the driver's seat.

D rode on without saying a word. Right behind him was Bingo on his horse, and Clay—who, not surprisingly, had climbed down to the ground.

"What, you boys going already?" asked the old woman. "I was just about to go deliver the girl to her home. Say, before I do, why don't we have ourselves a drink?"

Clay alone looked back at her. When he saw the figure that lingered by Granny's side like a white bloom, his ferocious face was suffused by a wondrous peace.

Perhaps noticing him, Tae lowered her head a bit.

Cupping his hand by his mouth, Clay coarsely shouted, "Hey, missy! I'll be seeing you! It was a fun trip. Oh, and Granny—I'll be sure to pay you back for making him go rescue me that time."

"Okay, but I'm not gonna hold my breath waiting on it," Granny said, both her voice and form dwindling in the distance, as did the form of the girl by her side. No one noticed that the girl watched the back of that black long coat for ages, her eyes hinting that it was the most dazzling thing she'd ever seen.

Wasting no time, D rode down one of the main streets and dismounted in front of a three-story building five blocks away. There was no sign of the Bullow Brothers; the town of Barnabas had a population of twenty-five hundred. As far as the buildings went, most were made of wood. Only after D had disappeared through a doorway did the first hopeless sighs escape from the dazed women who stood paralyzed in various parts of the street.

Just inside the door was a staircase, and to the right of the stairs hung a brass plaque engraved with the names of tenants.

Room 202: Thornton Law Offices. A black-gloved hand rapped on the door in question, and it opened right away. A young lady—apparently the secretary—froze there with her lipstick-rimmed mouth agape.

"Oh, don't mind her—c'mon in!" a voice the Hunter had heard before called from beyond the entryway.

Gently pushing the woman aside, D slipped through the waiting room and opened the door.

The room was of moderate size. Behind the desk by the window sat Thornton, a sullen look on his face. "Welcome. Right on time. But what else should I expect from Vampire Hunter D?" The lawyer offered his hand, but then reconsidered and withdrew it. Many Hunters avoided shaking hands. It was a precaution against being caught off-guard.

"Tell me what I want to hear," D said softly.

Thornton's condition had been that he cross the desert and reach this location by a designated time—which was this morning. Now it was time to collect on the other half of the bargain.

"You aren't going to ask how I was able to get here before you?" asked Thornton.

"No," the Hunter replied, "Although there aren't many who can operate a flyer."

The lawyer nodded, saying, "I happen to be one of them, though. So, how was your trip?"

"Where did you meet him?" asked D.

"You should ask him that yourself."

For the first time a hue of emotion surfaced on D's face. "Where is he?"

"He's in a certain run-down house on the southern edge of town. A long time ago, it was a Noble's mansion. It's all overgrown with weeds, but it seems he chooses his lodging based less on present appearances, and more on past glories. He should be sleeping at this hour."

D turned around.

"Wait. I was merely conveying a message for him. Nobility or not, he is my client, you know. Why did he have you cross the desert?" Thornton asked, but his words merely crumbled as they met D's back.

As the secretary watched him go, her mouth dropped open once more.

Thirty minutes later, the Vampire Hunter showed up at the dilapidated mansion. Across from the entrance, where even the bronze had crumbled with age, lay a hall as vast as the sea.

"Watch yourself," his left hand said. "He's here. I can feel him."

And, almost as if to overshadow that remark, a solemn voice said, *So glad you could make it.*

The source of that comment was clear. Halfway up the grand staircase that curved into the feeble darkness from the far end of the hall there stood a ghostly figure.

Crossing that desert was to be a trial for you. Not one of combat. What you witnessed was the end of something.

There was a flash from D's left hand, and three streaks of white light zipped through the black figure. As the rough wooden needles were swallowed by the darkness behind him, the figure smiled silently.

What did you see? What did you think? What of your own future? Do you still intend to subject yourself to day after merciless day of this? Do you not yearn for a life of peace?

D ran without making a sound. The rotten boards couldn't take the impact of a pebble, but as D dashed across them he didn't leave a single footprint. The Hunter cleared the first twenty stairs in just two bounds. He sprang—then slashed.

As the blade came straight down from above, the figure made no attempt to dodge it, but simply let it come. The blow passed through him without meeting any resistance.

This is your answer, then? Very well. That is what makes you my only success. But so long as you embrace that fate, death will ever cast its shadow over you.

Once again, D's blade shot up from below, slicing the steel banister in two.

"It's no use," the voice in his left hand said. "This is just some residual image from the past. Quit it already."

The shadowy figure leisurely receded up the staircase.

About to follow him, D was suddenly struck by a strange sensation—like he had just awoken from a dream. A single bound took him down the staircase, and the world grew hazy. Now D was in a dream. If the dreamer awoke, it would all disappear. The power to manipulate dreams was truly incredible.

D's left hand stretched out before him. A black line shot out toward the door. Even that rectangular region was distorted, but the instant it burst open to reveal blue sky, the door returned to reality.

Leaping out into the overgrown garden, D looked over his shoulder. The house behind him suddenly vanished, and a few prismatic orbs of light drifted toward him. Dreams. The orbs themselves were purely dreams. Anything they touched turned to dreams and faded away.

The black thread snagged a globe of light in midair. A second later, D drove his blade into the stain spreading across the surface of the globe, and the substance of the dream shattered to pieces.

"Outstanding!" a sleepy voice could be heard to say from the overgrown grass. As the swaying figure got to his feet, his legs wobbled unsteadily.

"Where's your brother?" asked D.

"In a saloon."

"Who put you up to this?"

"Didn't you know already?" Bingo said drowsily.

His body was pierced by a needle that scorched through the air, and then vanished as it still jutted from his flesh.

"When I dream, I am a dream," Bingo told the Hunter, laughing in his sleep.

Being real, D couldn't carve up a dream; at that moment Bingo was essentially immortal.

"I put a hole in your dream," D said softly.

Thin flakes of dark red fell like dust from his opponent's chest. The black lines that had flown from the Hunter's left hand were thin trails of blood.

"Shall we do this another day?" Bingo said calmly. As he slept, his serenity only seemed natural. "You can name the time."

"I'll leave that to you," D replied.

"Okay. Early tomorrow morning, then. Dawn is at four o'clock. So, right here at three-thirty."

"Why don't you make it during the day?" the Hunter inquired.

"Why don't you cut me down right here and now?"

The guard on D's longsword clicked home as the Hunter sheathed his weapon.

Pointing a slowly swaying hand in the direction of town, Bingo said, "I'll be in a bar called El Capitan all day long. Stop by if you like."

Night came. The wind that had been blowing out into the desert changed directions, carrying the grains of sand back to town. As they struck the windows and wooden fences, they made a lonesome hum. It was a melancholy sound both for those it saw off on departure and those it welcomed back on arrival.

It was late that night that Granny Viper called on D as he slept in the overgrown garden of a mansion. He ended up there after the hotel had refused to give him a room.

"Tae didn't come by, did she?"

Those were the very first words out of the old woman's mouth, after she'd called out to D in a shrill voice and followed his voice back to him.

"If she didn't come with you, then she's not here."

Granny sighed dejectedly. "A fine mess this is. Running off the very same day she gets here, the little fool." The old woman took a seat on the ground. Her shoes were white with dust. There was no light save that of the moon.

"What happened?"

According to what Granny told D in answer to his question, when the girl called on her brother and his wife, things didn't go so well. Her sister-in-law heaped abuse on her, determined from the very start to drive her away. *You're the Nobility's plaything,* she'd sneered. *Why couldn't you have just died somewhere along the way? It was my mother-in-law and father-in-law that asked them to look for you, not me. If you hang around, they'll burn our house down.* Tae's older brother said nothing as he simply watched his sister walk away.

"There's no reason to be so upset," D told the crone. "You must've imagined this would happen. Besides, your job is done when you deliver someone."

"That's true," Granny said, shrugging her shoulders. "But, you see, even I worry about what becomes of my merchandise from time to time. Why, I even swung by the saloon and asked those boys if they'd seen her. Well, I don't know about the older one, but the younger one ran out like I'd lit a fire under him. He's probably still looking for her now."

"If she comes by, I'll contact you. You're at the hotel?"

Granny mumbled something once again about the girl's stupidity, how she couldn't restrain herself for even a single day. Compared to how tough she'd have it trying to make it on her own with a dhampir baby to look after, a little verbal abuse should be music to her ears. Saying she was heading out to look for the girl again, Granny took off.

"A dhampir baby? Yeah, a dhampir . . ." she muttered, the words growing fainter and fainter until they were like a whisper through the trees.

A short while later, someone called out, "D!"

The pale figure appeared between the trees in the distance. By the time the figure reached the Hunter, he could see that it was Tae.

"Granny told me what happened."

"I . . . I really was going to put up with them," the girl stammered. "No matter what they said about me. But . . . when they called the baby inside me a vampire . . ."

"It's a dhampir."

"It's the same thing to everyone else!" The tracks of tears remained on Tae's cheeks, but no sparkling beads could be seen. She'd run dry. Held captive by the Nobility for eight long years, when she finally returned home she couldn't stay even one day . . .

"What will you do?"

"Let me rest here just for tonight," Tae said, her tone firm for the first time. Her single-minded gaze met D's eyes. "Come tomorrow, I'll manage something on my own. Just until then. Please, just let me stay with you."

"Do as you like."

Tae seated herself by D's side. He dropped a blanket in her lap.

"But this is yours . . ." said the girl.

"It's not for you."

Tae gazed at the blanket and then back up at D. A tear fell from her cheek, splattering against the back of the hand that held the edge of the blanket. Her supply of mournful tears had nearly been exhausted.

"Okay," Tae said as she pulled up the blanket.

"You said you'd manage something on your own, didn't you?" D asked as he gazed straight ahead.

"Yes."

"Well, there'll be two of you soon."

Tae didn't know what to say.

"It seems dhampir children are quite considerate, although there are exceptions."

While the young man seemed as cold as ice, a faint hint of a smile skimmed across his lips. Tae watched with utter disbelief and then sheepishly touched D's chest with her pale hand. D didn't move.

"I . . . I'll try to be brave," Tae mumbled, bringing her cheek to rest next to her hand. "Good," she said after a little while. "I can hear the sound of your heart. When I was a little girl, Papa told me something. He said dhampirs didn't breathe. And so their hearts didn't beat. I honestly believed him. That the Nobility had hearts of gold and veins of crystal, and that dhampirs did, too. Now I know that's not true, though after seeing you, I sort of thought it still might be."

D said nothing.

"But I'm glad it's not. A dhampir's heart beats just like ours. Your blood is warm, too. I'm glad. My baby will be just like you, won't it?" Tae said. She was crying. And she went on crying. Her voice was full of joy. Without knowing why, Tae thought that somehow she'd get by now.

At some point the girl lapsed into the quiet breath of sleep, and D had a puzzling look in his eye as he gazed down at her. A lock of hair had fallen across her forehead. His left hand reached out and stroked it back into place. Then he raised his face and stared off into the darkness before him.

A trio of silhouettes suddenly appeared. It was Granny and the Bullow Brothers.

"I'll look after her tonight," D said.

Granny twisted her lips at that, and Clay snapped in a deep voice, "You've gotta be shitting me! Would anybody leave a girl alone with a sex fiend like you in the dead of night? Behind that iron mask of yours, you're just looking for some fast action, you bastard!"

Her eyes shifting from the girl to D, Granny said, "It just occurred to me—isn't this going to wake her up?"

D's left hand came to rest of the back of Tae's head, and then came away again quickly.

"That won't be a problem now," the Hunter told her.

"I see," Granny said with a nod. But it was unlike the nod she always gave. "I think that rather than having the two of them live in misery, it'd be better for one of them to lead a regular life. You know what the best thing to do would be," Granny said, her right hand going for the jar on her hip. "You know, my sand paintings can even picture the insides of a person. I'm going to do this," the crone said, her voice trembling. But the quavering only served to make the strength of her resolve all the more apparent.

Gently setting Tae down on the ground, the Hunter in black slowly straightened up again. "Leave her alone," he said. Though his tone didn't hold so much as a hint of a threat, it froze not only Granny, but the Frontier's greatest warriors as well. D's eyes were glowing deep red—the color of blood.

"See . . . You see that?" Granny said, the words spilling from her trembling lips. "Would you look at your face now? That's what Tae's kid will be like, too. No matter how handsome he might be born, or how much stronger than a human being, in the end he'll always show that face. And every time he does—mark my words—every time it happens, everything he's managed to build up 'til then is finished. Not just once or twice. *Every time.* How many times have you worn that face so far? How often have you had the face of a Noble?"

"Leave her alone," D repeated.

"No, I won't stop. You may be a dhampir, but you're a man. How could you know the least bit about how a woman feels?"

The bloody hue rapidly left D's eyes. Staring at Granny, his expression was calm as he said, "You're a dhampir, aren't you?"

Time seemed to stop.

Granny was mired in a perplexity she couldn't begin to conceal. "What?" she exclaimed. "What do you mean?"

"Back in the desert, Clay came to lead you and me away. But Lance and Tae he carried off asleep."

"Pure coincidence is what that is."

"There's more. Except for the first glance you caught of the marker I set up on the grave, you wouldn't look at it at all. Because it's a shape you have trouble with. And why is it that when you came here earlier looking for the girl, your shoes were white with dust but you weren't breathing hard?"

D stared at her. The silence following the question was a hundred times more fearsome than any enraged shouting could've been.

Granny shook her head feebly from side to side. "Lies," she said. "You're making this up . . ."

"I have one more piece of evidence I couldn't have made up." D dealt the coup de grace.

"What . . ."

"The hatred you have for dhampirs. Only another dhampir feels that strongly."

"Stop it!" Granny exclaimed. As she shouted, she raised her right hand high in the air. Sand billowed from between her fingers.

A shot rang out.

The crone's right hand was thrust as high as it could go, and the sand in it scattered vainly in the breeze.

As he watched D dash toward the falling crone, Bingo called out, "Clay!" His voice may have been sleepy, but his orders were sharp.

"I'm on it!" Clay replied as his massive form vanished in the direction from which the shot had come.

There was never a second round fired.

D inspected Granny's wound; it went right through her heart. It must've been the work of a firearm of some sort. While it wasn't exactly a wooden stake, surely the only reason she was still alive was because she was a dhampir.

"D—" the old woman rasped.

"Don't speak."

"Don't boss me around." Granny took a shallow breath. "Don't know who the blazes did this or why, but there's no saving me now. That's okay. Let me go. And don't you dare think about waking up the girl. I wanna go out smooth. Say, would you mind holding my hand for a bit?" And as soon as Granny said that, she grabbed hold of D's hand herself. "Come on, it's not like we've got a lot of time. Ah, just as I thought—a cold hand. That's okay. It's a dhampir's hand. There's not much anyone can do about it. Oh, it's been decades."

D looked down at her face, the paleness of which was evident even in the darkness.

"You know . . . I had a child," Granny said with a laugh. "The mother was a dhampir, so her son was bound to be one, too. That's why my man ran out on me. I must've worked ten times as hard as anyone else bringing up my boy. If he had to be a dhampir, I wanted him to at least have a good dhampir life. But in the end there wasn't anything I could do. The night before his wedding . . . he went and sank his fangs into the throat of the girl he loved and was set to marry. Cried tears of blood, I did."

Granny turned her gaze toward Tae.

"Looks pretty while she sleeps, doesn't she?" the old woman remarked. "Tonight may be the last night for that. You know, other people always used to tell me the same thing. They'd say they'd never seen anyone look so hurt and angry in their sleep. It shouldn't be that way. I never wanted her to have to go through what I did. I still don't think what I was about to do was wrong. There are dhampirs who live like you do. Well, maybe I was in the wrong after all . . ."

Suddenly, Granny's complexion became more pallid.

"Oh . . . goodbye . . . Looks like peace is mine at last," the old woman said, her head dropping sharply to one side.

D peered down at her.

"Ah, that's right," Granny said as she opened her eyes. "I forgot to ask you to say some last words to me. Don't worry, I'm not asking you to tell me you love me or anything. Just say something."

"The girl's child won't run off."

"Is that a fact?" Granny said, breaking into a smile. "Great . . . If you can guarantee me that, everything will be fine." The old woman laughed heartily, and her head lolled to one side. After that, she moved no more.

Putting his hand to her temple, D folded her wrinkled hands on her chest.

"Is she dead?" Clay asked. He was standing next to his brother again.

"What about our duel tomorrow?" Bingo asked.

"Push it back to noon," the Hunter replied. "I've got a funeral to attend."

"If we've gotta postpone it, we could make it for the same time the next day instead."

"Think your employer would want that?" D asked, gazing at Bingo. Bingo turned to Clay, but Clay looked away. "Tell him I'll be paying a call on him a little past noon," D said in a bloodcurdling tone, and then he turned to Tae.

Tomorrow the girl would have to start her life all over again. But for now, her breathing was serene as she slumbered.

At noon the next day, a black carriage set out from a funeral parlor on the edge of town. Carrying the coffin, it would typically make its way through the major streets of Barnabas, with those in mourning for the deceased walking along behind it. Relatives, friends, and acquaintances alike had a chance then to bid farewell to the departed. Apparently, the person being buried that day didn't have a peaceful death. The driver of the carriage was still a young lady, and the lone mourner in tow was a gorgeous young man in black raiment.

There were remarkably few people on the streets in the strong light of midday. Those who were there watched the lonely funeral procession suspiciously. Ordinarily, even townsfolk who had nothing to do with the deceased would join the procession—that was simply Frontier courtesy toward those who died without family around. But not a single soul did so today. The previous night, certain facts about the nature of the driver, the deceased, and the lone mourner had blown through town like a hurricane. And the woman who'd whipped up that storm had left town early that morning with her husband.

Out in the white sunlight, there was no sound save the creaking of the wheels on the black carriage as the woman and man went by. The girl had lowered a black veil over her face, and the young man held his wide-brimmed traveler's hat over his heart. An almost imperceptible wind tousled the hair of both.

Before long, the procession passed by a three-story building. In one of the rooms there, three men were looking out the window.

"Perfect timing," the lawyer Thornton said, snapping his pocket watch closed with a crisp sound. Looking back at the men behind him, he said, "The time necessary to report Granny's death, the criminal investigation, and the arrangements for the hearse were all taken into account—there's no better time than high-noon for the dead to make that final journey. Don't you think so?"

There was no reply. Bingo Bullow and Clay Bullow—two of the Frontier's greatest warriors—looked rather displeased as they stared at their employer's back.

"Statistics say that for a dhampir, doing battle in broad daylight means a 40 percent drop in combat effectiveness. Don't look so unhappy," Thornton told the brothers. "It's not like I wanted to have to do this, either. Hell, if she hadn't been the grubby little people-finder she was, I don't think I would've used her like this at all. But to be perfectly frank, this all springs from your failure to get rid of him out in the desert."

As the lawyer needled him in that sore spot, Clay shrugged his shoulders. Bingo was looking down at the floor—though, of course, he was neither deeply impressed nor conscience-stricken.

"Desert crossing or not, this job isn't done until you kill the Hunter. And until then, I don't get my due, either. See to it you kill him today for sure." With these words, Thornton shut his eyes— one had to wonder just what sort of compensation he'd requested. The lascivious and arrogant expression he wore was unique to a

certain sort of person, and it spread across his face like an oily film. His plump hands lovingly massaged the back of his own neck.

Clay leaned forward a bit. The creaking of the approaching carriage had reached the second-story window.

"Well, now. This warrants full marks for effectiveness—he certainly looks like he's in pain. It would appear I haven't lost my knack for judging characters. Not only is the Hunter seeing her off at this hour, he's actually got his hat off, too. It only goes to show you can't believe all those rumors you hear about some people being heartless and cold."

The two brothers silently watched the passing carriage.

"You could take him now. Go to it," Thornton said, his voice vested with a strength that would brook no resistance.

Turning their backs on him, the pair walked toward the door.

Coming out of the building's entrance, the Bullow Brothers went right out into the street; the carriage and D continued to move along about forty feet ahead of them. The pair walked quickly. At a point about two yards from D, they slackened their pace. Neither D nor Tae turned around. Both brothers took off their hats. Holding them gently to their hearts, they followed along behind D. Now there were three mourners.

An hour later, the carriage halted at the communal cemetery out behind the same funeral parlor where its journey had begun. The gravedigger and undertaker were waiting by the hole they'd already completed. The group gathered around the grave, the coffin was lowered into the earth, and the undertaker began to recite a prayer. It was a short one. Tae chewed the words over in her mouth.

The ceremony ended, and the gravedigger began shoveling dirt back into the hole.

"Well, then," Clay said in a way that suggested the time had finally come to square accounts. "There's an open spot over that way. Let's settle this there."

"I just don't get it," Bingo said in a sleepy tone. "The night we first met, we were ready to kill you . . . But to be honest I really don't feel much like doing it now."

D started walking straight ahead. He got the feeling he heard Tae's voice.

Leaving the rows of gravestones, the trio squared off in an almost circular section thick with grass. They were ten feet apart.

"I have to thank you," said D.

"What for?" the smirking Clay replied. Making a massive leap away, he went for his harp with his right hand.

D made a dash for Bingo.

As proof that his foe had expected as much, the sleeper spat dream bubbles from his mouth. But spitting was exactly what D's left hand did, too. Strings of black blood attacked the cloud of bubbles with the suppleness of a whip, but slipped between them. The bubbles had skillfully avoided the attack.

"Good work, bro!" Clay howled. As long as Bingo was locked in battle with D, he couldn't let his deadly ultrasonic waves fly, but it looked like his older brother was doing pretty well.

Dodging the bubbles that came at him, D flung strings of blood at Bingo from his left hand. A new dream glittered into being in the sunlight to meet that attack. Every bloody thread broke against the surface of the bubble—blocked off completely. But once that bubble was gone, Bingo's expression showed agitation for the first time—his face filled with a forced vitality. Having spit up all of his dreams, the dreamer had awakened.

Using a melody of unearthly beauty to change the black shape that hung high in the air for a second like a mystic bird to dust, the younger Bullow gave a shout. Dazed, Clay then swayed unsteadily as he saw the naked steel that protruded from his brother's back. It'd dawned on him that what his harp had destroyed had merely been the Hunter's coat, just as D had raced across the ground and impaled his brother. His fingers went for the strings as his warrior training made him prepare a second attack reflexively, but then he stopped dead. D was on the far side of his brother. A split second of indecision—

As Clay stood there, a wooden needle whined through the air and sank into his forehead, dropping him. Due to the time necessary to extricate the Hunter's blade, Bingo didn't hit the ground until after his younger brother.

Two corpses lay in the white sunlight. The battle was done.

The wind blew by. For a time, D gazed at his two foes. Suddenly, he ducked as something hot whizzed over his head, followed by the delayed report of a gun. It came from the direction of the graveyard.

Crouched down and about to sprint into action, D heard a faint melody slip past his ear.

A cry of agony arose in the graveyard.

When D turned and looked down, Clay was lying there smiling. His harp trembled at the end of his outstretched hand.

"So . . . does that even the score?" Clay said, blood spurting from his forehead as he spoke.

"It was more than enough," D replied.

"Was it . . . really? Well, here's some interest on it. The guy that hired us . . . was Thornton. And that character just now . . . was another one of his killers."

"I know."

"In that case . . . let's finish this . . ."

The warrior's harp rose, then swiftly fell again.

"My luck is crap," Clay said, and then he closed his eyes.

D turned around.

Tae was standing there. That was why Clay hadn't used his harp.

The girl's face was pale with fright.

"Scared?" D asked.

"Yeah."

"Don't let your child become a Hunter."

"That'll be up to him or her," the girl replied in a trembling voice that was charged with power. "But even if my baby doesn't grow up to be a Hunter, I'll raise him or her to be like the Vampire Hunter I saw."

"It's almost time for your ride to leave," D said as he took a quick glance at the sun.

"You give me money and buy me a ticket for a coach . . . and there's nothing I can do to repay you?"

"Just see to it that I hear rumors that you're doing well."

Tae's eyes sparkled. "I'm sure you will," she said with a nod. Taking a bundle of white fabric from the bag she carried, she unfolded it. It was a tiny garment to swaddle a tiny life. "This is what I made on the sewing machine," Tae said, as if lost in reflection. "Now I have a feeling I'll be able to get by somehow. And it's all thanks to Granny. She did nothing but help me, and we weren't even kin."

"I still have business here in town," D said as he gazed at the girl's face. "Godspeed."

"You take care, too." Tae watched as he turned his black back to her and went off into the white light. Her womb was filled with the movements of the tiny life within her, and felt warm. Just as they parted, she'd seen a smile rise on D's lips. And for a long, long time after that, through days of intertwining joy and sadness, the girl would recollect how she'd been the one to put it there. She would tell the tale to her only child with a touch of pride. It was just such a smile.

Postscript

How did you enjoy this *D* novel? It's hard to believe we're already up to the sixth book. Actually, 6 is my lucky number, and if you put two more 6's after that, you wind up with *The Omen.* (Laughs) Of course, if it'd get me that kind of power, I wouldn't mind putting those extra 6's on there. (Laughs)

Well, as this is my third new postscript in a row, I thought I might talk about how the Vampire Hunter D series came to be. My debut as a novelist, *Demon City* (*Shinjuku*),was published in September of 1982, and because it sold fairly well, the publisher asked me to get to work on another novel right away. At the time, something about vampires popped into my head as the prime book candidate—although it would be more accurate to say that I had wanted to do a story about vampires for my first book. The reason I ended up going with something else first was because the theme of vampires seemed to be much too specialized, and, up until that time, there really hadn't been a book intended for a juvenile audience that dealt with such grotesque material. Most likely, a horror tale written to illustrate the terror of the protagonist as he or she is menaced by supernatural forces would've been poorly received by young readers (males in particular). In order to avoid that pitfall, I introduced action into my debut novel. It is an indispensable element in stories for younger readers, and since I'd always liked action myself, it was almost inevitable that I'd wind up writing books like this. What's more, I decided to include more elements of science fiction in my new novel. The reason for this should be obvious: young people seem to prefer sci-fi to horror. (Although the reception horror receives may differ in this respect between Japan and America.) At that time, no one here had written a novel like *Demon City*. It proved to be the birth of what I later termed "horror action." Fortunately, it got results—and because the sales were good, the editorial staff had no complaints when I said I wanted to go with vampires.

Basically, I grew up watching movies about Japanese ghost stories; Hammer Films from England like *Horror of Dracula* and *Curse of Frankenstein*, and Universal offerings from America such as *Dracula* and *Frankenstein*. I had but one complaint about monster movies, and a wish to see it remedied. I always thought, "Instead of having these monsters and ghosts just beating the hell out of everybody non-stop, wouldn't it be great if there was a hero who had even greater strength than they did?" After all, who likes losing all the time? To be perfectly honest, my novels take a lot from the best points of horror movies. The setting of *Demon City*, where Shinjuku has been cut off from the rest of Tokyo by a massive earthquake, is very similar to that of the John Carpenter film *Escape from New York* and the Japanese manga *Violence Jack*. Also, the protagonist of Vampire Hunter D is reminiscent of the titular character of the Hammer Films movie Captain Kronos—Vampire Hunter (though D is about ten thousand times more handsome than the actor who played the lead in that movie (laughs)). And D's also naturally patterned after the leading character of the classic *Horror of Dracula*, who scared the life out of me when I was nine or ten—Count Dracula, as portrayed by Christopher Lee. Despite the fact that I found Count Dracula to be a creature that should obviously be destroyed, and regardless of the fact that at the time I was more enthralled with Peter Cushing's role of Van Helsing than I was with the vampire he kills, the utter coolness of Count Dracula dressed in black and standing at the entrance to some beautiful woman's room was something I couldn't overlook simply because he was the villain—it had a great impact on me. D's hallmarks—being distant, tall, and garbed in black— were all traits borrowed from Lee's Dracula. In other words, you could say D is like *Horror of Dracula* embracing the trappings of *Captain Kronos*.

Having the hero be a man of peerless beauty wasn't actually a matter of my own personal tastes, nor was it a ploy to secure female readers—it was to make his coolness perfect and complete. Furthermore, D is burdened with the fate of being a dhampir—a human/vampire half-breed. Until now, I've always said the reason for this was because a purely human hero would've been boring, and also because having D be both human and vampire—but shunned by both sides—only served to intensify his tragic nature. But the simple truth is that I really wanted to try and give him some of the wonderful vampire characteristics from Lee's excellent portrayal of Dracula. And that's how D was born.

Next time, I'll try to touch on D's world and his partner after a fashion, "the left hand."

Pilgrimage of the Sacred and the Profane is one of the great books in the series as far as the color and development of the cast of characters are concerned. In particular, the two heavies were my favorite characters, and I still regret only using them in this one volume—it seems like such a waste. Incidentally, there's a scene near the end that's borrowed from a certain American movie, and I wonder if my English-speaking readers will know what film that is. No one in Japan ever caught it.

Hideyuki Kikuchi
June 28, 2006
while watching *Billy the Kid versus Dracula*

And now, a preview of the next novel in the
Vampire Hunter D series

VAMPIRE HUNTER D

VOLUME 7
DEMON JOURNEY TO THE NORTH SEA
Part One

Written by
Hideyuki Kikuchi

Illustrations by
Yoshitaka Amano

English translation by
Kevin Leahy

Coming in May 2007
from DH Press and Digital Manga Publishing

A Vision of Beauty

CHAPTER I

I

After midnight, the wind grew stronger. The clouds rumbled as they rolled along. In accordance with the moon's dips into that cover, the night alternated between glowing with white light and sinking into pitch blackness. Somewhere out there, something howled. A cry unlike anything she'd ever heard, it made the girl by the window grow stiff.

"Nothing to be scared about," said the master of the lodging house, wiping his mouth after another in a long line of drinks of cheap booze. The unlabeled bottle of what seemed to be home brew had been nearly empty of liquid, and was filled instead by a dark green surprise: a frog. In these parts, various species of back-leaping frogs were used to bring a full-bodied taste to the liquor. But even though this lodging house was near the northernmost extreme of the Frontier, it was still difficult for travelers to ignore the local practice. "That right there's the sound of beast weeds blooming. We don't get many dangerous critters in these parts."

Perhaps put at ease by this, the young woman turned from the window and smiled. It was a lonely little smile that suited the seedy lodging house, although the seventeen-year-old brimmed with a beauty that saved her from seeming too gloomy. Even the dreariness of her shirt and slacks, waterproofed with animal fat, seemed unable to counter the charm lent to her by the silver comb stuck in her red hair.

Out of the collection of five rest houses that made up this unbelievably small community, this was by far the most squalid. There was no one in the brick hall save the innkeeper and three patrons, including the girl. But add two more people, and the room would've been completely packed.

"How far you going anyway, miss?" the innkeeper asked as he turned his liquor bottle upside down and shook it.

"To Cronenberg," the girl replied.

"Now, I don't know where you hail from, but it's a hell of a thing for a lady like you to choose this of all roads. If you were to take the main road instead, you'd get there a whole lot sooner."

"It'd be a whole lot more dangerous, too. Wouldn't it?" the girl said, covering the leather pouch attached to her belt with the palm of her hand. "The road from the Belhistan region to Cronenberg, in particular, is swarming with monsters. I'd rather not run into any mecha beasts or mazers or any of those types, thank you." Though her tone was colored with loathing, there was no fear in it.

While the back roads that branched off from the main thorough-fares had less danger from monsters, they were beset by natural disasters such as landslides, quicksand, and impasses, as well as plenty of human monsters—thieves and bandits of all sorts. Traveling alone, especially for a girl at her tender age, wasn't something to be undertaken unless you were quite fearless and well-skilled in the use of weapons. And though the girl's facial features still shone with the innocence of youth, one could catch a glimpse of a resolute will in them as well.

"Well, if you've come this far, there's just a bit further to go—you should be there by tomorrow evening. Get yourself a good night's rest. Fortunately, summer's almost here. The road's pretty rocky, but I suppose the season will make it a touch nicer."

At the innkeeper's appropriately slurred words, the girl got a faraway look in her eye. "Yes, summer," she muttered. "At last."

At that moment, someone beside the reinforced lacquer door said in a hoarse voice, "Florence."

The girl spun around. Surprise tinged her eyes.

"Yes, I thought as much," the voice said with apparent satisfaction.

The girl noticed then that the speaker sat with the electric lantern on his tilting wooden table turned off, melding with the darkness. Despite the fact they were in a house that was all closed-up, the man wore a wide-brimmed hat as well as a woolen cloak. Although the gray hair and beard that hid nearly all of his face testified to his age, the eyes with which he watched the girl brimmed with an uncommon vitality.

"There's no reason to pull such a face," the old man told her. "It's a simple deduction, actually. You have the smell of salt and fish about you, and the comb in your hair is made from the bones of a lion fish, is it not? That's a local specialty. If you grew up in Florence, I'd warrant you have all the pluck you'd need to travel on your own. If you'll pardon my asking, just what manner of business sends you to Cronenberg?"

The old man's eyes gave off a light that seemed to draw her in, and the girl had to turn away.

"Aw, look what you went and did. Now the little lady's all pissed off," the final voice in the room said, rising from another window directly across from the girl. The speaker was a young man, and he'd been the very last to come down from one of the rooms upstairs. Though his look of fearless determination fit his muscular physique, the pale line running diagonally across his right cheek couldn't help but lend another impression—a less than reputable one.

All present took in the young man's face, but their eyes quickly shifted to his hands. Perhaps the sight of them had stimulated their hearing, for they now heard the sound of the little things sparkling between the fingers of his meaty hands. Squinting her eyes, the girl realized that it was a pair of thin metal rings.

"Care to give it a try?" the man asked, grinning as he held out his right hand to her. The rings were shaking. To the man by the door he said, "You don't ask anyone where they're from or where they're headed—that's the rule of the road. For starters, you haven't even given us your name. I guess as people grow older, they get all inquisitive and such, do they?"

"I wouldn't know," the old man said, shrugging his shoulders. "But I suppose it was impolite of me not to introduce myself. You may call me Professor Krolock. It's not an official title, mind you."

"I'm Wu-Lin," the girl said with a bow. It was an ingrained reaction.

"I'm Toto. Anyway, how about a little wager, missy?" the young man suggested. "It's a simple game, really. All you need to do is separate these two rings. Like so."

Reaching for the loose end with his other hand, the man—Toto—pulled in either direction. The rings came apart without any resistance at all, but no matter how closely Wu-Lin scrutinized where she thought she'd seen them separate, she couldn't find any opening or break. Toto quickly put his hands together again. And the rings were back the way they'd been.

"You get three minutes. The bet is for one gold kraken coin."

Wu-Lin's eyes bulged in their sockets. "Those are worth five times their face value on the Frontier," she said in disbelief. "There's no way I'd be carrying that sort of money."

"Good enough. For something else then," Toto said, his smile strangely affable. "What that pretty little hand of yours has been safeguarding the last few minutes."

Startled, Wu-Lin twisted her body to put her waist out of Toto's view, but at the same time two more pairs of eyes concentrated on her from another direction. They were focused on her pouch.

"You're looking awfully pale . . . it must be rather important to you. If it's not cash, I'd say it's jewels . . . or maybe a youth elixir?"

And with that, Toto suddenly got a serious look in his eye again. "Well, if it's all that precious to you, I won't twist your arm. Whatever money you've got will be fine. I'll still put up one kraken coin. And I'm a man of my word."

Wu-Lin's expression shifted. Judging from her wardrobe and her current accommodations, she wasn't exactly traveling in luxury. Kraken coins were produced in extremely limited quantities and were quite valuable. That one coin would be enough for her to hire an armed escort and pay for a carriage all the way to the Capital.

"Relax," the young man said. "Even if I clean you out, I'll at least buy you some breakfast tomorrow morning. Once you've eaten your fill, you'll make it to Cronenberg somehow or other."

His smiling face and equally affable objections served to strengthen Wu-Lin's resolve. "I paid for my room in advance, but that only leaves me with four coppers," the girl confessed.

"Well, that'll do," Toto said, spinning the silvery rings around his fingertip. "Okay, here's mine."

His left palm went down on the table, and then came away again. The glitter of gold was reflected in all three pairs of eyes.

Taking a seat in the chair across from him, Wu-Lin lifted the lid of her pouch and thrust her right hand into it. Her left hand kept it covered so no one could see inside. The faces of the four copper coins she produced were covered with a patina.

"That's the spirit!" Toto said. "You get exactly three minutes." Handing the two rings to the girl, he gazed at the magnetic watch around his wrist. "Ready—Go!"

As he gave the signal, Wu-Lin focused her entire being on the rings in her hands. On closer inspection, one of them did have a break in it. But while it had an opening, the gap wasn't half as wide as the other ring was thick—it was as thin as a thread. But Toto had got them apart. Relying on her memories of what she'd seen, Wu-Lin tried every possible movement with her hands, but the rings remained hopelessly linked.

"Three minutes—time's up!"

As Toto spoke, the girl's shoulders—which were quite solid for a girl her age—fell in disappointment. Setting the rings down on the table, she let out a deep sign.

"I like you, missy," the young man said. "You're not gonna raise a stink and call me a cheat, are you?"

"If I did, would you give me my money back?"

Toto broke into a broad grin. "Sure, why not? I'm not about to give you my coin, but you could walk away with your own. All you'd have to do is give me one little bitty peek at what you got in that pouch."

This seemed to be quite a generous offer, and after furrowing her brow for a moment, Wu-Lin soon nodded her agreement. She probably figured since he already knew she was carrying something precious, there was really no point in hiding it. Hers was a rather decisive temperament.

"Hey, you guys better not look. This is just us gamblers squaring away a debt," Toto coldly told the other two men as he watched Wu-Lin's hand disappear into the pouch.

Her hand came right back out. In it was a wad of black velvet. Brusquely setting it down on the table, Wu-Lin pulled the shiny black cloth to either side without pretension.

"I see," Toto said, pursing his lips. Rather than being impressed, he seemed a bit suspicious—and more than a tad disappointed.

There lay a semitransparent bead that Wu-Lin could've easily concealed in the palm of her hand. Essentially a sphere, it was marked in places by faint distortions. While the material from which it was crafted was unclear, judging by its dull silver glow, it didn't appear to be any sort of jewel or other precious stone.

"Satisfied?"

"What the hell is it?" Toto asked.

As he reached out with one hand, Wu-Lin quickly jerked the bead away. Carefully rewrapping it, she said, "It's a kind of pearl."

"It came out of the sea, did it? So, I guess you came all this way to sell it, then. I hate to break it to you, but that thing—"

"It's no concern of yours," Wu-Lin said flatly. Quickly picking up her coppers and putting them and the velvet wad back into her pouch, the girl returned to her seat by the window—back to the sound of the wind, and the ever-changing hues of the darkness.

At that moment, there was a dull sound off in the distance—the thunder of hoofbeats. They were drawing closer.

The innkeeper set down the glass he was holding. "No one passes this way at this hour," he said. His voice was stiff.

"It's a traveler," Professor Krolock said, his eyes still shut.

Toto stopped toying with his rings and muttered, "In the dead of night? They'd have to be funny in the head."

No sooner had he spoken than a beastly howl drifted eerily from the opposite direction of the hoofbeats.

"They're out?!" the innkeeper practically screamed as he got to his feet. "It's those damn bronze hounds! They run in packs of ten or so. Can't do squat to them with a sword or spear."

"We've got to let whoever it is in!" Wu-Lin said, dashing toward the door, but the innkeeper raced over like the wind and grabbed her tightly.

"Oh no you don't," the innkeeper said. "It's too late for that. If those accursed hounds get a whiff of humans, they'll be in here, too!"

"But—" Wu-Lin started to protest, but she caught herself.

The cramped room was filled with the sort of silence that made the flesh crawl. The sound of the hoofbeats continued to steadily grow louder, and then they seemed to pull aside in front of the door, even though the rider had surely heard the hounds.

A different sound arose from the end of the road: the clatter of countless paws scampering closer.

"We have to help that person!" Wu-Lin swung her foot forcefully, and the innkeeper grabbed his crotch. The girl ran to the door.

"Don't do it!" Toto shouted from behind her, but even as he did, she was reaching for the doorknob.

A split second later, the girl turned right around with her hand still extended and dashed back across the room. Stopping in front of the counter that served as both the bar and the front desk, Wu-Lin was frozen stiff in amazement, but the rest of the group didn't get to see it. For at that very instant on the other side of the door—right in front of the lodging house—two kinds of footsteps collided, and the night was filled with the howling of beasts.

Wild dogs with hides like blue steel made straight for the poor traveler and his horse. A bladed weapon swung down at the beasts, only to bounce off them in vain. Flesh-rending fangs and blood-spattered muzzles—it was a tragic scene any of them could easily imagine, but a second later it was over. The howls of the bloodthirsty beasts were suddenly cut short, and the thud of one heavy body after another hitting the street echoed out—and then silence . . . or almost silence. There was only a hard, faint sound steadily fading in the distance. The sound of hoofbeats.

No one moved, or even said a word.

After a little while, Toto got up and quickly walked over to the door.

"Hey!" the innkeeper called out in a voice that was tiny and hoarse. He could only imagine what had transpired outside.

Toto roughly threw the door open. The warm nocturnal air was heavy with the scent of aromatic night grasses. The wind struck Toto in the eyes but couldn't tarry there, and the young man caught another of the night's scents.

The moon was out. On the road, the scenery was a stark contrast of black and white—but black seemed to be the stronger of the two.

The smell was coming from a number of pools of blood. The heads and torsos of the bronze-covered wild dogs had already ceased twitching.

"One, two, three—" Toto said, extending a finger with each number. "Exactly ten of the beasts! And all of them put down in less than two seconds—"

Leaping out into the road, Toto gazed in the direction the hoof-beats had gone. The howls of the night wind made his well-trimmed hair and the hem of his coat billow in the same direction.

"It might've been *him* . . ." the others in the doorway heard Toto mutter as he faced the darkness that swallowed the end of the road. "He can travel by night. And all alone."

II

Early the next morning, Wu-Lin left the lodging house; she didn't even bother to eat. The innkeeper and the other guests were still asleep, and the eastern sky was just beginning to shine with a watery light. Dressed in the same clothes as the night before, she was shouldering a vinyl backpack.

After walking for three minutes, the girl reached the edge of town. Beyond the fence, a cedar so huge it would take three men to get their arms around it stretched up to the blue sky. In this region, it was customary to grow enormous trees on either side of the main road through town. It was hoped that doing so would bring the community some of the same mysterious vitality the trees possessed. Further past that massive tree, the rows of cedars continued.

Opening the gate and then shutting it again behind herself, the girl was just about to walk off when someone appeared from behind the trees.

"Professor Krolock?" Wu-Lin said.

A gray-haired head bobbed at the receiving end of her tense gaze.

"Good morning, young lady. Off to an early start, I see." Placing one hand on his chest, the professor bowed elegantly.

"So are you," Wu-Lin replied. "I wouldn't have thought you'd be out before me."

"Actually, I couldn't get much sleep. At any rate, if it pleases you, would you accompany me to Cronenberg?"

"Are you headed there too, Professor?"

"Actually," the old man said, "I am. My carriage is parked behind yonder tree."

"You sure I wouldn't be intruding?" Wu-Lin said, staring intently at him in his scarlet cloak.

"Whatever could you possibly mean?"

"Why ask me way out here?" the girl inquired.

"I might've suggested it back at the lodging house, but there was a certain boisterous individual around."

"And you wanted me all to yourself?" asked Wu-Lin.

"Precisely," the old man replied, a smile forming on his lips. "Approaching you in town was going to be troublesome, so I simply waited out here. I wouldn't be so cruel as to say I don't care what happens to a young lady like yourself. Please, join me. All I ask in payment is that bead you have in your possession."

"I thought as much. I guess it's a good thing I showed it off so no one got too curious and slit my throat while I slept." Wu-Lin then asked the old man, "Do you know what it's worth?"

"Probably better than that rabble last night," the professor said, closing his eyes and nodding to himself. "But, as yet, I don't have a good idea of its true value. To really ascertain as much, I'd need you to hand it over to me."

"Sorry. I'll travel alone." As if in jest, the girl bowed exactly as the professor had, and then a second later she sprinted off like the wind.

Not bothering to chase after the girl as she swiftly dwindled in the distance, the professor muttered, "Such a tempestuous child," and thrust both hands into his cloak. What they came out with were very strange items indeed. His right hand held a quill pen; his left hand held a brownish scrap of paper—a dried piece of animal hide.

Returning to the tree and leaning against it, he raised his right hand. Without seeming to particularly conceal himself for the task, he took the sharp tip of the pen and stabbed it into his left wrist. Not even glancing at the gore that spread across his skin when he pulled it out again, he took the blood-dipped pen and began to draw something on the surface of the parchment—what looked to be a human face. After about ten seconds, the pen's movements ceased. Running his eyes over his handiwork at length and nodding with satisfaction, the professor then embarked on an even stranger course of action. Lovingly bringing his face closer to the portrait of darkening red, he began to whisper something in a low voice.

Having already run more than a hundred yards, the girl suddenly found her feet getting heavier. A hue of bewilderment rose in her face. While she didn't stop, she had noticed a rather odd phenomenon—her legs seemed to be gradually losing their strength, to the point where she couldn't run any longer.

"I—why is this happening . . .?" With those weary words, Wu-Lin squatted down right then and there.

Less than a minute later, a wagon drawn by a pair of cyborg horses rumbled along with a sound that hardly suited a road at daybreak, stopping right behind the girl as she crouched down, cradling her knees. It went without saying that the man who sat in the driver's seat holding a whip was Professor Krolock. The grotesque parchment was rolled up in his left hand.

From his lofty perch, the professor said, "You mustn't keep these problems to yourself. I'll be happy to hear them. Won't you climb into my carriage so the two of us might mull over your dilemma? Come."

All exaggeration aside, the old man's tone truly swam with affection. At the sound of his voice, Wu-Lin got up and began to walk toward the wagon without the slightest hesitation.

And then something equally bizarre occurred. The professor's right hand abruptly shot out, and with a sharp crack from his whip, the wagon made a wide turn toward town—back the way they'd come. Odd as it may seem, the professor who'd taken the trouble to follow Wu-Lin there then cracked the whip again and, scattering fragments of the dawn's light like dust and ice, started off in the opposite direction in a great hurry.

As the old man and his wagon vanished down the road, another figure stepped out from behind the trees that towered by the roadside. He was leading a horse as he came into Wu-Lin's paralyzed view. His right hand was clearly toying with a pair of gold rings that kept clinking together.

Waving his left hand before the eyes of the mesmerized Wu-Lin, the mysterious young traveler—Toto—made a wry face. "He calls himself a man of learning, and then he goes and puts some weird spell on a girl like you—that's really tempting the wrath of heaven. That said, I must confess I'm after the same thing myself. Don't take it too hard," he told the girl. "Looks like I was right when I guessed that bead was really something after all. Allow me to be of some assistance."

Wu-Lin seemed to have had the very soul drained out of her, and at this point a baby probably could've taken what it wanted from her. He tapped her pale cheek with his right hand as if humoring her. The man was reaching for her pouch with his left hand when something hot whizzed right by the end of his nose.

"There she is!"

"Don't let her get away!"

Not only could a cacophony of shouts and hoofbeats be heard coming from the direction of town, but the sharp whistles that came from the figures closing on the pair soon became steel arrows in flight.

"Just as I thought—we've got company! And here that old innkeeper was trying to come off so friendly and all. The world's a nasty place. Sorry, but this is where I make my exit," Toto said.

But as the young man's hand reached once more for the pouch, it was caught by Wu-Lin's. Just as the shock was altering Toto's complexion, his wrist was expertly twisted back against the joint and he was physically thrown a good ten feet down the road. And yet, the way he executed a skillful one-hundred-eighty-degree roll and landed lightly on his feet was certainly an eye-opening display of acrobatics.

"Hey! Wait just a second!" Toto shouted, but just as he was about to charge back to the girl, a number of arrows flew over his head. As he hit the ground despite himself, the sound of iron-shod hooves and excited shouts reached his ears.

A shadowy form leapt over his head. Needless to say, the rider holding the reins of Toto's cyborg horse was none other than Wu-Lin.

"Thanks for the horse. See you!" With that brief shout, the girl—who'd escaped from the professor's spell before Toto even realized it—slammed her right heel into the mount's flank and galloped away as fast as she could.

Riding for a full hour at breakneck speed, Wu-Lin was a few miles from an intersection with the main road when she finally let her horse rest its legs. It was an area still lit with the cold, clear rays of dawn. At any rate, she considered herself safe for the moment. She never would've thought those two men would be lying in wait for her, and it'd certainly been a mistake to fall under that mysterious spell, but since she'd managed to extricate herself from the situation, none of that mattered anymore. Having acquired a horse in the bargain, it was likely she'd reach Cronenberg at just past noon instead of in the evening.

Recalling the stunned look on Toto's face as she'd thrown him, Wu-Lin smiled innocently, but it took less than two seconds for that smile to freeze. The sound of hoofbeats was growing nearer.

She thought it might be the "professor," but there was no squeak of wagon wheels. What she saw were a number of horses—and racers, at that. They wouldn't be out delivering mail at this hour. Was it the last group that'd shown up as she was leaving?

Just as Wu-Lin was about to give a kick to her mount's flanks, something whistled through the air as it dropped toward her. Sparks shot up on the right half of the road about ten feet ahead of her, and a fierce shockwave knocked both horse and rider down on their respective sides. It was the work of a portable firebomb launcher. An expert could hit a target the size of a brick from more than two hundred yards away, but if they were only trying to blow something up, all they had to do was increase the amount of gunpowder.

Wu-Lin immediately got up. For the time being, her foes were only trying to slow her down. Fortunately for her, they seemed to be concerned about damaging the bead and they had adjusted the amount of gunpowder accordingly. As a result, the girl hadn't been fatally wounded, or even broken a single bone.

As Wu-Lin tried to get her horse back on its feet, she coughed and felt the urge to vomit building within her. In truth, she'd taken a blow to the stomach when she fell. Jamming a finger down her throat, she retched immediately. As she vomited, she realized her horse was a lost cause—its neck was twisted grotesquely. If it had been one of the models cherished by the Nobility, it would've continued to run even if the entire head had been torn off, but this one was intended for humans. Wiping her lips, Wu-Lin shouldered her bag and looked all around. The woods were thick to either side. Behind her, the silhouettes of riders formed hazily in the white light. She couldn't afford to hesitate.

Wu-Lin ran to the right—the woods might serve to restrict the movements of horses. The trees and bushes would probably provide her with some cover from the explosives as well.

Just when she thought she'd melted into the grove of the trees, an impact slammed into her from behind, and a sharp pain shot through her back—probably a branch, or a small stone. The next thing she knew, she was lying on the ground. Putting her strength into her limbs, she tried to get up.

Right behind her she heard a familiar voice say, "Give up already. We'll make it quick for you." It was the innkeeper.

Wu-Lin got to her feet without looking in his direction. About five yards ahead of her was a thick grove. *How many seconds would it take me to get there?* she wondered.

"We don't wanna blow that doodad of yours to kingdom come, you know. So we won't finish you with the mortar. What do you fancy, a sword or an arrow? Or would you prefer we garrote you?"

More voices than she could count laughed in unison.

Wu-Lin started to make a break for it, and then stopped. At the same time, the laughter ended as well.

Why is everyone always popping out from behind trees? Wu-Lin wondered.

The newest arrival was a dashing figure. He wore a wide-brimmed traveler's hat and a long black coat that sheathed his tall form elegantly. The longsword on his back had a graceful curve to it. For a second, Wu-Lin had to wonder whether it wasn't a moonlit night after all. But the reason she and the men behind her froze there was because unconsciously they knew that an aura of extreme danger lingered around the gorgeous stranger.

"Who the hell are you?!" someone asked, his voice quavering.

Wu-Lin swiftly circled around behind the figure's back. "Help me!" she cried. "They're bandits!"

The stranger didn't move.

"Out of the way, pretty boy," the innkeeper said.

There were half-a-dozen men on horseback—with the innkeeper leading the pack—and all of them wore vicious scowls. Surely their racket consisted of finding travelers with something valuable, then following them when they left and killing them. They were armed with swords and spears, but the man to the far right was the only one with disk-shaped bombs loaded into a crossbow-like launcher that he had pointed at the ground.

"Well, it doesn't really matter," the innkeeper said to the huge fellow to his right. "Now that he's seen our faces, it's not like we're about to let him live. We'll send him to his reward along with the girl." To the pair he added, "Just consider this your brief romance, and kiss each other goodbye!"

As she listened to his cruel words, Wu-Lin clung tightly to the back of the shadowy figure. But something suddenly became apparent. The man in black wasn't looking at the other men. At the end of his gaze was a grove of trees and sparkling green leaves. Between him and the other men faint beams of light swayed—sunlight peeking through the trees. Wu-Lin looked up at his profile; there wasn't a hint of sadness on his face. It put Wu-Lin's heart at ease.

Broadswords and spears glittered in the men's hands. With wild shouts, they charged the stranger.

Still, Wu-Lin remained entranced, enchanted by the beauty of this strange young man.

Hammering the earth beneath them, a pair of riders raced by the stranger, one on either side, and they kept right on riding with blood streaming out behind them. From the waist up, the riders no longer existed. Before the rest of the killers realized what had happened, the upper bodies of their compatriots were lying at the shadowy figure's feet. Bloody mists tinged the white sunlight.

When the startled man with the launcher readied his weapon, the figure kicked off the ground without a sound. The hem of his coat flickered like a dream.

A head flew. The innkeeper's torso fell in two distinct pieces.

Seeing what looked like the figure's chest being penetrated by spears thrust from either side, Wu-Lin cried out. But the shadowy figure was in midair now. What the murderous implements had pierced was merely his afterimage.

A circular flash slashed through the necks of the last two men. When the figure landed on the ground again, there was one more flash of light as he flung the gore from his blade onto the green grass, and then the weapon disappeared back into the sheath on his back. A head landed on the ground far off, and the rest of the body dropped off at the horse's feet.

The massacre had unfolded in the time it took to blink.

Dazed, Wu-Lin rubbed her eyes. The image she observed wasn't the least bit ghastly. The sunlit scene of carnage was like some shadow-puppet show.

It's his fault, she thought fuzzily. *He's so beautiful; he even makes death look good.*

The shadowy figure returned. His footsteps made no sound at all—he could walk across water without making a ripple. He was a young man. That was all she knew. The cool mood the tall man in black seemed to generate didn't allow the girl to return to her senses until he was in the middle of putting a saddle onto a cyborg horse that was tethered to a tree not far away.

Wu-Lin ran over to the stranger in spite of herself and bowed. "Thank you," she said. "You saved my life."

As the young man loaded what looked to be a sleeping bag behind his saddle, he asked, "Are you traveling by foot?"

Perhaps any other information about the girl and the circumstances surrounding that deadly battle didn't matter to the young man. They had attacked him, and he cut them down. Brutal as it was, that was a perfectly natural way to live on the Frontier.

"Yes," the girl replied.

"Use one of their horses."

"Um—" Wu-Lin stammered. Before she could say anything more, the man in black was on his mount. "Are you going with me?" she finally managed to say, but her words struck the stranger's broad back as he'd already ridden a few paces.

"I'm looking for somewhere to get some sleep."

Wu-Lin didn't understand his reply at all. The world was swimming in light.

"At least tell me your name. I'm Wu-Lin," the girl called out, her shouts blocked by the grove.

And then a reply came from the very same stand of trees: "D."

III

Cronenberg was a town that stretched across the plains one hundred and twenty miles north of the center of the Frontier. Although this small city, with its population of thirty thousand, was a far cry from the scale of the Capital, it was a place where goods were collected from all over the Frontier and thus kept the roads well-repaired; the community also maintained a decent level of activity year-round. There was cold storage for seafood shipped from the coast, vast processing plants for livestock that'd grazed on the plains, drying houses for vegetables and grains— and for the rest and relaxation of those involved in the transportation of all these things, and the guards that kept them safe from bandits and beasts, there were saloons, hotels, casinos, and women.

The chatter of men and women persisted all day long in the area where the drinking establishments could be found, but once dusk settled like a thin wash of ink, the multicolored lights grew brighter, and the strides of people on the streets got lighter. Because the number of monsters and supernatural beasts in this plains region was comparatively low, the streets were full of people from evening until the wee hours of the morning.

And it was at twilight that Wu-Lin arrived at the town. The cyborg horse she rode was one that'd belonged to the thugs D had killed in the woods. Asking one of the guards about a certain shop as he opened the gate for her, Wu-Lin then proceeded to the center of town.

While it was common for a woman to travel alone, it still came as little surprise that the remarkably untamed beauty of the girl's face and body drew the eyes of men on the street.

In front of a tiny little shop Wu-Lin dismounted. The sign had the words "Cyrus Curio Shop" painted in letters that were now almost completely blurred. Tethering her horse's reins to a pole outside, Wu-Lin went into the shop.

The dusty odor of old furniture reached her nose. Old-fashioned tables and chairs, paintings, sculptures, antique mirrors—the merchandise that rested in the murky light—differed little from what would be found in any such shop, but Wu-Lin wasn't there for the furniture. When she struck the call bell that sat on the counter in the back, a door that looked to be something of an antique itself opened, and a middle-aged man who was little more than skin and bones appeared.

"Welcome," the man said as he ran his eyes over Wu-Lin.

"There's something I'd like you to have a look at," Wu-Lin said, covering her pouch with one hand.

"Well, that's the line of work I'm in, so I guess I'll take a gander," the man replied in a less-than-amiable tone. "But unless it's

198 | HIDEYUKI KIKUCHI • VAMPIRE HUNTER D

something really spectacular, you won't get much for it from me. Especially not for curios—"

"It's not old."

"No?" the man remarked. "So you want an appraisal, then?"

"Yes."

Dubiously eyeing the package Wu-Lin opened in her hand, the man picked up the sphere. "What is it?" he asked.

"I don't know. That's why I'm here."

Shrugging his shoulders, the man then held the sphere up to his eye. "Where did you come by it?"

"Near my house . . . on the beach there."

The man's eyes shifted for a second to Wu-Lin. "From the sea?" he muttered. "You know, I can't tell much without really looking into it. Would it be okay if I kept it?"

"How long?"

"Let me see—till noon tomorrow."

"Could you write me up a receipt for it?" asked the girl.

"Sure."

Taking a form imprinted with the proper information from behind the counter, the man hastily signed it and handed it to Wu-Lin.

"Whereabouts are you staying?"

"I haven't decided yet," the girl replied. "I'll be back again at noon."

Pointing down the street, the man said, "Take a right down at the corner and you'll find a hotel. Quarters are cramped, but it's cheap and the service is good."

"Thank you," Wu-Lin said with a smile as she turned to leave.

Making sure she'd gone, the man went into the back room and set the sphere on the desk he used for appraising antiques. Taking a seat, he didn't use any of the electronic lenses or microscopes around him, but rather rolled the sphere around in his hand. Suddenly seeming to recall something, he looked up and smacked his fist to his forehead. Several minutes passed before the following words spilled from his lips: "So that's it . . . I remember now! I'm sure it was in that book . . . This is a Noble's . . ."

As the blood drained from his already corpse-like countenance, the man grabbed his jacket from the back of another chair, stashed the sphere in his pocket, and headed for the door with lengthy strides. What the man didn't notice as he reached for the doorknob was that his body had turned in entirely the opposite direction. With the same tense expression as ever on his face, he walked toward the window on the far side of the room with a much gentler gait.

The door opened behind him. And who should step in but Toto, cautiously surveying the room as he entered. Judging from the way he quickly walked over to the man and fished the sphere out of his pocket, he must've seen everything the shopkeeper had done since entering the back room. Giving a light tap on the shoulder of the man who thought he was still facing the door, the mysterious young man bounced the bead from his right hand and the pair of rings from his left in the palm of his hand. "Sorry," he told the shopkeeper, "but I'll be taking this. Kindly give my regards to the little lady. See you!"

With those words, Toto took off like a gust of wind. But even after he was gone, the owner of the curio shop just kept plodding slowly toward the window—although in his own mind, he thought he was hurrying toward the door.

About an hour later, several men went into a saloon. It was the one with the gaudiest neon sign of all of the drinking establishments that lined that bustling thoroughfare. Their fierce expressions and powerful bodies made it quite evident they were in a dangerous line of work. Heading straight to the counter in the back, one of them said something to the bartender, who then used the hand that'd been wiping out glasses to indicate a door far to the right.

"That little bastard—you've gotta be joking me," spat the man who'd spoken to the bartender, curses rolling from him like an incantation. When he tossed his jaw in the direction of the door, the other men started across the room with a brutal wind in their wake. A pair of muscular men who looked like bodyguards stood by the door, one on either side, but they let the group pass without saying a word.

Just beyond the door lay a hallway. There was a row of lewd pink doors on the green wall. Though no voices or other sounds could be heard, the men knew what was going on behind the bright pink planks, and it seemed like they could almost see the hot, dense fog rising from each and every door. After all, it wasn't at all rare out on the Frontier for saloons to double as whorehouses.

Stopping for a second, they checked the number plate above one of the doors, and then the whole group headed down the hall to the right. The door down by the first corner was their destination.

When they were a few steps shy of their goal, they all heard a woman's voice shout, "What are you doing?! I told you I'm not going for that, you lousy pervert!" At the same time, the door swung open from the inside. Along with the sweet smell of spices, something pale flew from the room. It was a half-naked woman, clutching her clothes to the front of her body.

"You bastard!" the woman shouted. Her sensuous face twisted into a demonic phiz, and she swung her right hand. Something shot back into the room, there was a dull thud, and then a cry of pain.

"Take that, you fucking deviant!" the woman roared before she growled to the group, "Out of my way!"

Watching the woman stalk away indignantly, the men were grinning at each other when they heard someone say, "Damn, that hurt! Where'd you run off to, bitch?!"

Spewing curses and groans all the while, a powerful form appeared, clad only in a pair of briefs. His right hand was pressed against his forehead, and he had a high-heeled shoe dangling loosely from his left. A pendant of two interlocked rings swayed against his hairy, muscular chest.

"I paid you a good chunk of change. The least you could do is indulge me a little. I'll grab your sorry ass and—" At that point, he noticed the men and said, "What the hell do you want?"

"Been a long time, hasn't it, Toto?" the man who'd spoken with the bartender said with nostalgia . . . only his eyes weren't smiling.

Staring intently at his face, Toto broke into a nostalgic grin, too. "Well, spank my ass, if it ain't Peres! This is some coincidence. Are you still doing the roving bodyguard routine?"

"Looks like neither of us has changed," Peres replied. "When I heard about what happened at the antique store, I knew it was you. Seems you're as good as ever with that trick of yours."

Toto was playing down his abilities as he reached for his chest, but his pendant jolted away right before his hand.

Staring thoughtfully at the rings he'd torn free, Peres forcefully suggested, "Let's talk inside."

Still rubbing the back of his neck, Toto replied, "First, I have to get that bitch and—"

But as he attempted to go out into the hall, there was a dull thud against his solar plexus. Doubling over with a groan, he was shoved roughly back inside by the man who'd just punched him.

As he fell in the center of the medium-sized room, Toto groaned, "What the hell . . . was that about?" His Adam's apple bobbed madly as he tried to take a breath.

"Check his clothes," Peres ordered one of his compatriots as he bent over Toto.

The room had no decorations, save a bed and an end table—the latter of which had Toto's clothes strewn on top of it. The glass window above the bed reflected the neon lights outside.

"You stuck your nose in a hell of a place this time," Peres said in a sinister tone. His eyes were laughing. "Though I don't figure you ever dreamed things would go like this. Without me around, Mr. Gilligan wouldn't have ever known about you, or the fact that you like this place more than three hots and a cot. Too bad, eh?"

"Who the hell is *that*?" Toto asked in a tone that was somehow calm, suggesting that his pain had subsided.

"Why, he's the big boss who runs everything here in town. That was a serious mistake, making a move on a curio shop he's connected to. I hear there's something unbelievable all tied into this. The boss went completely nuts and had us grab not just you, but the girl who brought it here to have it looked at, too. Hey, now," Peres cautioned Toto, "don't try and slip away. I know all your tricks. I know how tough you are, too, but these guys do this for a living. You don't want them taking you apart alive, I bet."

Having said his piece, Peres then turned toward the end table.

"It's not here," said the man searching through Toto's clothes. "Where'd you stash it? Your hotel?"

"Yeah," Toto replied with a pained nod.

"All right, then. We'll all go get it. But I'm warning you—if I find out you're jerking us off to buy some time . . ." Peres said, lifting the corner of his coat. A sheath with a broadsword hung against his leg. They were convenient items, and depending on what your needs were, they could be used for anything from butchering a fire dragon to skinning a man alive.

"Do whatever you like," Toto said as he stood up.

"Give him back his clothes," Peres told him compatriot, adding, "But only after you've torn all the pockets out."

A few seconds later Toto's garments were thrown back to him, and he quickly put them on. "What happened to the girl?" he asked.

"You worried about her?"

"Yeah . . . I know what a scumbag you are and how you like to get your kicks. You don't exactly take it easy on women or children, do you?"

"You'll just have to wait until we're in Mr. Gilligan's basement to see about that, I guess."

"Fine with me," Toto said, his body sinking.

Catching a vicious shoulder attack in the stomach, Peres flew toward the table.

"You little bastard!" the other men snarled, although the reason they all charged Toto immediately must've been because they knew he was unarmed. Perhaps that was all they had in mind as they attacked.

A metallic clink sound rang out.

Peres watched in a daze as his compatriots completely ignored their forward momentum and turned around sharply a mere foot shy of Toto.

"Where the hell did you have 'em ?!" he shouted as his right hand raced to his broadsword. Then suddenly his eyes went wide with a second surprise.

"Right here!"

The flash of silver that shot forth with Toto's words answered both of Peres's questions simultaneously.

Hacking half-way through the man's neck with his own blade, Toto spit something out of his mouth for the other man to see as his old acquaintance fell to the floor gushing blood: a pair of metal rings.

"Never showed you that before, did I? Don't go thinking things never change," Toto lectured Peres, whose head flopped to one side. He then dashed over to the window, threw it open, and leapt out.

He landed on the street along the left side of the saloon. The moon was now out. He crouched down momentarily when he hit the ground and then started running. To the rear there was a concentration of eateries. Avoiding them, he quickly turned right instead. The alley was full of shadows. He knew if he kept going straight, he'd come out at the grain storehouses.

As he began to put his strength into his legs, a crisp sound reverberated behind him. It was whistling. Toto became a statue. It had that sort of ring to it. Nevertheless, Toto managed to slowly turn around.

At the entrance to the alley he'd just gone into, a figure in blue stood illuminated by the moonlight. He was tall and wore a cape. A sword hung from his left hip, and the handle and sheath were both covered with exquisitely intricate carvings. Both hands wore leather gloves, and they hung naturally by his sides. And yet it was perfectly clear that they would flash into action in response to any possible movement. It was infrequent to encounter people like this. Perhaps he was one of the men after Toto, waiting outside as a precaution.

"What do you want with me?" Toto called out, his voice surprisingly calm. Surely he hadn't exactly led a normal, peaceful existence, either. "Are you with them?"

"Come with me," a gorgeous voice said. It was as clear and fresh as the moonlight.

"What for?"

"Because you're the suspicious character I saw break open a window and run away. I'm taking you to the sheriff's office."

"Spare me. C'mon, pal. From the looks of you, you're no more than a step or two removed from my world yourself. Just let me go, okay? As a favor to another guy."

His reply: a whistle.

A certain feeling suddenly filled Toto's heart. It was that sort of melody. And the instant it completely filled his ears a flash of white mowed through Toto's abdomen, and his body was blasted by a lust for killing.

Toto somehow managed to jump. However, as he hung in the air, blood spread from him like smoke. When he landed fifteen feet away, a grotesque mass of intestines spilled from his belly with a gush of blackish blood.

Toto couldn't believe it. The distance between him and the man with the drawn blade in his right hand was at least fifteen feet. Now, there was less than six feet between them. How had his opponent closed the other nine feet?

Something hot welled up within him. No longer able to bear it, he began coughing. More than just gore splashed out in the alley. Even covered with dark blood, the sphere retained its dull shine as it bounced once on the ground and then gingerly rolled across the alley.

Just behind the bead, Toto finally noticed another alley to his right that lay wide open. However, he never had time to see this new path as an escape route. Pinning him to the ground with the sheer ferocity of his will to kill, the gorgeous man calmly drew closer with his naked blade. There was no doubt in Toto's mind that any movement now would only invite a deadly blow. With desperate eyes, he gazed down at the puddle of blood at his feet— the pair of interlocked rings was in there somewhere. He heard whistling. When it stopped, the moment of fate would come. The melody flowed on . . . and then faded away. The blood seemed to drain from every inch of Toto. And then there was nothing left.

Toto looked up at his foe, but his opponent wasn't looking at him. His gaze was concentrated on another alley.

Following the other man's eyes, Toto found it was now his turn to be astonished. There was a man's face so gorgeous it could make even someone caught in hellish agony lose himself. He saw something darker than any ordinary darkness—a darkness given human form that hovered at the entrance to the alley. It was a vision of beauty. That was the only way he could describe it. The face beneath the traveler's hat melded with the darkness, but had he been able to actually see it, the sight might've left him breathless with sheer envy. He wondered if perhaps it was some spell that the night put on him that caused these two gorgeous men to appear before him in that narrow alley.

The second figure bent over and picked up the bead. He left himself so wide open to attack that it looked like a mere child could cut him down. Gazing at the bead, he asked, "Is this yours?"

"Yes, I'm sorry to say," Toto replied. And as he spoke, he took the intestines lying in the road and began stuffing them back into his abdominal cavity. "See, someone gave it to me. You know, I hate to do this, but I have a favor to ask of you. I have to be running along now, but I was hoping you could help out the bead's owner. And I'll let you keep that as payment. Seems it's really worth a hell of a lot. Although I do have to warn you, I'll be along later to take it back from you. You'll find her in the basement of the house that belongs to a scumbag by the name of Gilligan. I'm counting on you, pal."

And saying that, Toto leapt away to the rear. While it wasn't clear exactly what the secret of his physiology was, his strength was unbelievable. The whistling figure didn't follow him.

"What will you do?" he said. It sounded as if the moon had asked the question.

There was no reply.

"You plan on going?"

"We'll see," the new arrival said, responding for the first time.

The whistling figure continued, "You're even better looking than I am—and I've never met a man like that before. What's more, I believe I know your name: Vampire Hunter D. I may as well introduce myself. The name is Glen. I'm a seeker of knowledge."

He received no reply.

"Once again, I'd like to know if you intend to go or not."

D's outline melted into the darkness.

Glen looked up at the sky. Dark clouds were blindfolding the moon. When they cleared, there was no sign of D.

"I guess you went," Glen muttered in a low voice.

After a while, the melancholy whistling faded off into the moonlit distance.